*About Apollo Africa*

The original Heinemann African Writers Series was launched in 1962 with the publication of Chinua Achebe's *Things Fall Apart*, Cyprian Ekwensi's *Burning Grass* and Kenneth Kaunda's *Zambia Shall Be Free*, with Achebe himself acting as an editorial advisor. Over the next 40 years, the series continued to publish the best writing from across the African continent.

One of the founding aims of the Heinemann series was to make books by African writers available to as wide a readership as possible. Apollo Africa – a collaboration between Black Star Books and Head of Zeus – is proud to continue this work, ensuring novels, essays, poetry and plays from the original series are once again made available to readers all over the world.

*The Grub Hunter*

# The Grub Hunter

*Amir Tag Elsir*

Translated by *William M. Hutchins*

*Black Star Books and Head of Zeus would like to thank the following organisations: The Miles Morland Foundation, The Ford Foundation, and Africa No Filter. This publication was made possible through their support.*

First published in the Heinemann African Writers Series in 2012 by Heinemann Educational Books

This edition published in 2023 by Black Star Books and Head of Zeus, part of Bloomsbury Publishing Plc.

Copyright © Amir Tag Elsir, 2010
Translation © William Maynard Hutchins, 2012

The moral right of Amir Tag Elsir to be identified as the author of this work has been asserted in accordance with the Copyright, Designs and Patents Act of 1988.

All rights reserved. No part of this publication may be reproduced, stored in a retrieval system, or transmitted in any form or by any means, electronic, mechanical, photocopying, recording, or otherwise, without the prior permission of both the copyright owner and the above publisher of this book.

This reprint is published by arrangement with Pearson Education Limited.

This is a work of fiction. All characters, organizations, and events portrayed in this novel are either products of the author's imagination or are used fictitiously.

9 7 5 3 1 2 4 6 8

A catalogue record for this book is available from the British Library.

ISBN (PB): 9781035900657
ISBN (E): 9781803288772

Typeset by Siliconchips Services Ltd UK

Printed and bound in Great Britain by
CPI Group (UK) Ltd, Croydon CR0 4YY

Head of Zeus Ltd
First Floor East
5–8 Hardwick Street
London EC1R 4RG

WWW.HEADOFZEUS.COM

For Faisal Tag Elsir

And his yams and colourful worlds

If you wish to question your reflection
Some warm night
When your eyes are closed and the query's on your lips,
Don't search for yourself in the mirror,
For that would be a silent dialogue; you won't get any response.
Amble, instead, down to the street and search
Among all the people;
Here you'll find everyone, even you.

*Spanish Song*

*Chapter One*

I'll write a novel. Yes, I will.

This is a really strange idea for a retired secret police agent like me. I'm Abdullah Harfash, or Abdullah Farfar as I've been known since I was young in the neighbourhood where I grew up; this handle has stuck with me all my life. Actually, writing a novel isn't such a strange idea, because recently I've seen in some newspapers and magazines I've got hold of and read at my leisure that a Bengali who sold roses in the French city of Nice wrote a novel – about roses. The heroine was an African migrant who bought red roses from his shop for twenty years, without ever choosing another colour. The florist imagined that she was sending the roses to a sweetheart she had lost in a hideous war. A poor Rwandan cobbler composed a novel about the interethnic civil war in his poor African country, one that not even the men who started the war had ever written. A reformed prostitute in Saigon also wrote two brilliant novels: one about her former life when she was a nobody in a dark alley, and the other about her new life after she founded a small factory that makes mint candy.

Now her novels have been translated into every language, and readers are dazzled by them.

But how did I get this strange idea? I've never been a reader, and my imagination is limited, except for practical matters. I've never previously stood in front of a bookstore – unless I was shadowing a suspect who entered one, or following up on police reports about banned books smuggled into the country by professional gangs and sold under the counter. R.M., a Christian who owned A'laf, one of the old, established bookstores in the capital, and who became my friend because I kept him under surveillance for so long, once gave me a book, which was translated from French, about magic and magicians' feats. I spent days thumbing through it but didn't derive any genuine enjoyment from it – not even when I read about the Indian magician Rajendra, who once entered a chicken coop and emerged as a braying wild ass with stripes. The Jewish girl Nira Azamonde drank a hundred rotls of castor oil without suffering from diarrhoea, vomiting, or a hernia. The well-known Nigerian magician Hajj Boko disappeared from an enormous crowd he was entertaining on a street in Kano, and then was seen by many people minutes later performing the lesser pilgrimage. Clad in pilgrim's garb, his head shaved, he circled the Ka'ba in Mecca with them. From the bookstore of this same Christian – R.M. – I once confiscated fifty copies of a contraband book, amazed that so many copies of this book, which dealt with marriage practices around the world, could have entered the country. I won't deny that it interested me a little and that many of its stories appealed to me – especially the account of proposing to a girl by suddenly lifting her skirt above her knees. This was said to be customary in some African tribe. I would walk along the street imagining that the skirts of many passing girls were raised and that I had done this to propose to them.

No doubt the origin of this idea can be traced back in some way to that freak accident, the one that cost me my right leg and my job, which I valued and really enjoyed. For a number of months afterwards I was confined to my house, which I only left when it was absolutely necessary.

We were on a stake-out – at least that was what it was called when we received our orders. My colleagues in the National Security Agency and I enjoyed missions like this because we wouldn't need to move around, race through the streets, or conduct any interrogations. We just sat in the back of an open vehicle parked at some dark corner and watched the road. Intelligence had been received that suspicious meetings were being held at a farm in the southern suburb of the capital. Its owner, the entrepreneur S.J., was a prominent iron merchant. We didn't know what was really happening at that farm, or whether this actually was a threat to public security or merely an ordinary morals charge. If the culprits were normal men and women, a public security investigation wouldn't be warranted.

Early that night we parked our vehicle at the foot of a

hill near the beginning of the road that led to the farm. I was accompanied by two other agents. One sat quietly behind the steering wheel, and the other was in the back with me. Our two walkie-talkies, which were made in China, were turned on, and we could hear gibberish from headquarters streaming out of them. We used them to transmit information about developments or to receive orders, when there were orders that needed to be relayed. I had my eyes fixed on the road, gazing at its emptiness. My colleague A.B. was busy fooling around with his mobile phone, skimming through text messages and laughing for the tenth time at a joke he had received in one of them. It concerned an Iraqi woman whose husband was absent from home for an entire day. Since she had no idea where he was, she wept non-stop, thinking that he had left her for another woman. Her mother comforted her: 'Be optimistic, girl. Perhaps there was an explosion either in the market or where he works, and he died.'

Suddenly we saw the fleeting lights of a vehicle coming from the direction of the farm and heading towards us at high speed. My comrade, who cut short his eleventh shrill burst of laughter, and I were dismayed. I yelled into my walkie-talkie to tell headquarters about it and ask what to do. We set off after the vehicle immediately and powered our way up the hill. Our headlights illuminated the road, revealing pebbles, sand, and two scrawny nanny goats stumbling around in the dark. I don't know exactly what happened, but the other vehicle, which was a red limousine, suddenly made a U-turn and headed back the way it had come. Our open vehicle flipped over, strewing its contents – me, my colleague A.B., and the driver – over the hillside's sharp pebbles, and I lost consciousness.

The driver died in that freak accident. My colleague A.B. was afflicted with uncontrollable tremors and lost his memory, which he has never regained. I lost my right leg, which was amputated in the military hospital because gangrene had set in. Subsequent reports confirmed that the red limo leaving the farm belonged to another security agency that didn't coordinate with us. Its mission had priority over ours because the driver outranked us. He was working undercover, attempting to disrupt the conspiracy from within. We had spoiled his mission, which had been poised for success without our knowing anything about it.

I wasn't married and had never thought of marrying at all, even though in my time I had met dozens of girls, who may well have filled houses with chatter and children by now. I had no brothers or sisters, and my only aunt, Th., who lives near my house with her husband, the masseur for a sports team, came to help me when I was first disabled, before I obtained a prosthetic leg. My aunt took on chores like moving me about, feeding me, and washing and ironing my clothes. Her whole body trembled whenever she noticed a weapon gathering dust on the table, heard the radio blaring nonsensically in a language she didn't understand, or saw my pathetic handwriting on one of the yellow papers on which I loved to draft reports. When I was finally able to move about by myself and pursue my new life without anyone's assistance, Aunt Th. disappeared, claiming that the lower back pain she had once suffered had recurred because of all the bending she had been doing. She left me to contemplate the huge void sketched on all my surroundings. I thought all the time, and strange ideas that would never have occurred to me but for this void began to haunt me.

I will write a novel.

This idea was insanely persistent; I couldn't put the kibosh on it. It persisted some more, and I still couldn't quell it. I will no doubt write that novel. I'll struggle hard to learn how to write novels. I'm no less important than the Bengali florist who sold roses in Nice or the poor cobbler in Rwanda, and my sins may be comparable to those of the former prostitute. I'll write two novels: one about my former life with two sound legs, and another about my current life with a wooden leg. To avoid upsetting myself, I won't use the word 'sins' and will speak instead of 'experiences . . .' Yes – many, varied experiences. How shall I begin?

Scratching my head nervously, I stumble upon the answer after deep reflection. Yes, I know now where I'll start.

*Chapter Two*

I approached Qasr al-Jummayz, the capital's oldest, rowdiest, and busiest coffeehouse, which also serves as an expo of suspicious characters, at least seen from our professional perspective – that of our daily reports, which we draft with a strange glee. Here you find established authors and other folk who are struggling to achieve a status that seems out of reach to them. There are dapper poets wearing trousers and splendid shirts, barefoot poets who don't even have torn sandals, desperate journalists, and politicians. Everyone is smoking, talking gibberish, vying with one another, and sketching for their audience a nation unlike the one we inhabit, know, and love – with all its qualities and defects. Women are always hovering around the clamour or helping to fuel it with multiple discharges of laughter, which in our security reports we characterise as the chortles of vipers.

My right leg, which was manufactured locally from very smooth wood, hampers my ability to get around, but I have grown used to its weight since it was made for me, and now it follows when I lead. After a little practice I have learned to cover several kilometres with it, walking at a moderate pace. I'm able to squeeze with it onto buses packed with poverty and people, and once even swam in the Nile for two whole hours without it causing me any problem. I counted that a huge triumph. I remember the first time I entered the ancient coffeehouse. I was just beginning my career – a rough young man trained to extract the elements of a conspiracy from even a breeze, the wings of a fly, or smiles. Back then I was assigned to shadow the late A.S., a political activist who belonged to a banned party. He was a great windbag, and masses of people would congregate around him, even if he were babbling at the bottom of a well. He was known to recruit poor and marginalised people, drill them in the language of insurrection and revolt, and enlist a large number of them in his banned party. Then he suddenly fell silent. He would walk silently down the streets, greet people and acknowledge their greeting silently, come every evening to Qasr al-Jummayz, where he sat silently in a remote corner, and then leave silently. Officials of the National Security Agency interpreted his silence as a shameless conspiracy against the fatherland and felt that it inevitably portended dire consequences unless we nipped it in the bud. That particular day, I found him sunk in his profound silence; he hadn't touched the full cup of tea before him or his water pipe, which had gone out.

I tracked that silence and embedded myself in it for hours until he left the coffeehouse. I continued to follow it and imbued myself with it for more than three years, delivering to my superiors a daily report filled with the most sophisticated interpretations of this silence that my limited imagination could devise – until the man suffered a fatal heart attack, without leaving in our notebooks a single pertinent syllable. Even so, I was honoured the day he died, and my mission was deemed a success.

Qasr al-Jummayz (or the Sycamore Fig Palace) was filled with customers at that hour. The old sign with peeling letters had been replaced by a new one, resplendent with colour, decorations, and neon lights, after the elderly founder died and his heirs sold the coffeehouse to one of the new entrepreneurs. I didn't find any of the former waiters – men like Antar, al-Shafi', or Speedy Rambo, who had become as renowned as the coffeehouse and had attracted customers to it in the past. I discovered instead spotless young women – refugees from Ethiopia, which was experiencing a meltdown at the time – clad in dark brown uniforms. Their hair and eyelashes were tinted brown, and they welcomed patrons in broken Arabic that left their lips reluctantly. With delicate, tender hands they served coffee, tea, incense, and regional sweets, or provided a live coal for a water pipe that had gone out. One of these waitresses welcomed me with an enticing greeting. She wanted to guide me to a remote, isolated corner since she had noticed I was alone, but I was searching for the novelist A.T. and wanted to sit at his table, which – as I knew from previous surveillance when I was tailing various politicians – he rarely left. Perhaps I would gain some insight on how to begin the project that obsessed me: writing a novel.

This author, who had been a luminary for many years and whose name was always being mentioned in the media, fortunately was present that day. He was sitting by two tables, which had been pushed together, at the centre of a rather large group, most of whom were elegantly attired women who wore makeup and addressed him respectfully. One of them was describing his latest novel – *Eva Died in My Bed* – as one that the jinn had helped to write, since a mere mortal could not have penned it. Her statement was no doubt intended as a huge compliment, but I took it as criticism. The luminary, A.T., sat up straight, raised his head, and smiled in a way I did not find especially enchanting, even though it enchanted the others, and then declared, 'That's right! Yes, writing by the jinn.'

My knee-jerk reaction was rage at having been forced to retire after my leg was amputated due to the accident in which a fellow agent lost his life. In the past, an affair like this wouldn't have ended with a smile and a head thrust back arrogantly. I would have gone searching for Eva, who had died in a bed that was almost certainly stuffed with intrigues and conspiracies. I would have torn off its sheets, pillows, and covers and dragged this idiot to another destiny. But I soon calmed down. I wasn't on an official mission. In fact, I'm no longer affiliated with any security agency. Instead I'm seeking a way to write a novel. Apparently, this is how novels are written and then praised as crafted by the jinn rather than by human beings. I repeated the novel's title to myself several times to be sure to remember it and vowed I would get a copy later from the Christian R.M. or some other bookseller in order to learn how Eva died on one of their beds and what else was involved. Perhaps this would serve as my introduction to writing, or I might imitate the novel and produce something that would boost my morale. I was very close to the world of writing now; the wooden chair I had dragged from an empty table and pushed among those at the luminary author's table seemed very close to the man's chair. With some scrutiny I could glean from this arrogant face, which was beaming confidently, many reactions that might assist me once I became a luminary like him and people flocked around me. No one paid any attention to the ruckus I made by moving the chair and attempting to edge closer to the writer. They were all too swept up in their rapture to care. The woman who had said that the jinn had helped write the novel appeared to be opening her lips again. She asked, 'But, Master, where did you get the idea?'

A.T. leaned back in his chair then, to create space for the question to make the rounds of all their minds – or so it seemed – before he sat up straight again. The questioner kept her eyes trained on him while he relaxed and then tensed his muscles. She was a young woman of a type we classify in our security folders as a rash girl capable of poking her foot into a beehive, knowing full well it's full of bees. In the past it would have been very easy to follow her and write dozens of verbose reports about her conduct and appearance. The faded blue jeans that she wore and that delineated her body with stunning clarity seemed to violate common decency and to constitute a severe provocation for a stern verdict from the judges of the Public System – either prison or a whipping. I would not give much thought to her identity now that I was out of the service. I would pursue my personal mission: that of learning how to write.

The author declared, 'Plot ideas are present at every time and place, my friends. Actually they are present even in our lungs when we breathe, and in our intestines when we digest food, on the public road, in TV ads, water jugs, the meowing of cats – in everything. But many of these ideas are lost because they fall into the hands of shifty instead of gifted people. I have a laundry list of novels that would have been much better if I or some other special person had written them – Arabic, Chinese and Japanese novels, or even ones from the Comoros Islands. All the same, the idea behind *Eva Died in My Bed* isn't an ordinary one. It puts life and death together in one bed, where they sleep together under the same blanket and wake together the next morning. I wrote that novel approximately two years ago after returning from a trip to Moscow. I'm still proud I wrote it and fear I'll never write another novel as good.'

This was an extremely difficult statement. I couldn't understand how thoughts could exist in the intestines, which are designed to digest food, or in a lung designed to breathe, a water jug, or a cat's meow. Life and death covered by a single blanket, sleeping and waking together? Writing must be harder than I had thought when the idea that I should write a novel started to obsess me. Perhaps it's some chronic, incurable disease. Those writers must be madmen needing someone to treat them or to put them in asylums where they and their ideas can be isolated from the rational world. My eyes scrutinised the people gathered around him as I searched for looks of concern prompted by his recondite words, but no dismay was visible – just more admiration. The woman who had asked the question was smiling profoundly now. From her leather bag, which was scuffed at the edges, she pulled a huge manuscript wrapped in rose-coloured paper and handed it to the writer after rising from her seat and displaying her inspirational body.

'My first novel . . . *A Moment of Love* . . . would benefit from your introduction, Master. I finished it just yesterday and feel sure you'll like it.'

A.T. didn't seem too thrilled but took the manuscript from her; she was adorned at the wrist with a pewter bangle and on the thumb with a ring featuring a green gemstone. He cast a pessimistic glance at it and placed it on his lap. He didn't thank her, and I gathered that he regularly received manuscripts like these from novice authors. They probably annoyed him more than they made him feel flattered as a sought-after writer of prefaces. I thought that once I've written my obsessive novel, I'll present it to him in a similar wrapper and watch his pessimism and disgust. But my novel certainly won't be a love story like the novel by the woman who wears faded jeans and asks questions. Even though I'm not a cultured person, I believe that this type of story no longer impresses anyone, because love has now become a daily routine practised even by beggars and homeless people. My novel is different – even if all I know about it is that I'll write it very soon.

One of the Ethiopian waitresses lunged at us – the same girl who had greeted me seductively and tried to lure me to a remote, isolated corner. She placed a live coal in a customer's water pipe that had died out, released a barrage of smiles that clearly expressed her vexation and forbearance, and then departed. I discovered that I was clearing my throat forcefully in order to ask a weighty question I never would have thought I would put to a luminary writer surrounded by his infatuated admirers.

'What rituals do you observe when writing, Master?'

The word 'rituals' was totally new to me; I don't remember ever using it before. I don't know how it leapt to my mind at that moment.

I was suddenly besieged by all their faces, even the writer's, which I thought, at that moment, resembled a she-camel's. I don't know why a she-camel's face as opposed to a mare's or anything else. They were scrutinising me with interest, looking up at my face and down at my foot. Some of them may have felt a certain anxiety about a stranger appearing among them at a session where they knew exactly who did and did not attend. They must have noticed my wooden leg, which my tunic didn't successfully conceal, despite the garment's length. The girl in faded jeans trembled visibly as she looked away, off into the distance. I noticed that her grey polyester blouse was throbbing violently on the left side of her chest.

'Would you kindly tell us your name?' A.T. asked.

'Abdullah Farfar. I mean Abdullah Harfash. "Farfar" has been my handle since I was young.'

'Your name and handle are both inspirational, Farfar-Harfash.[1] Are you a writer?'

They were all so focused on me then that one man burned his fingers with his cigarette and a girl wearing a short, violet, linen tunic opened her knees and forgot to close them. I felt proud having attracted the attention of cultured people seated at a culture table. If only I really had been a writer, I could have brought out my book just then to sign with my old Parker pen, which I had filled with ink, before handing copies to everyone while enjoying their envious glances at the cover. But my novel would definitely be written one day, and I would sit at this table or a similar one in another coffeehouse. Then someone

---

[1] Both *Harfash* and Farfar mean something like 'guttersnipe', but this sarcastic comment is also a reference to the use of the plurals of these words as the titles respectively of the novel *Al-Harafish* by Naguib Mahfouz and the play *Al-Farafir* by Yusuf Idris.

would enter with a wooden leg, artificial eye, or decayed teeth to inquire about my rituals for writing and where I got my plot ideas. Perhaps a girl, dressed in a way that violated common decency, would hand me a love story in need of a preface. I would receive it dourly and not thank her. A.T. had relaxed now and closed his eyes as if picturing his rituals in his mind before revealing them to the assembled throng.

'I've made a stab at it, Master.'

'Excellent, veteran of writing stabs.'

Finally he opened his eyes. 'My writing rituals differ from one text to the next. I write some novels while elegantly attired and seated in the lobby of a swanky hotel or the departure lounge of some airport. Some texts I compose naked in a closed room with the drapes drawn and not a breath of air. Some texts won't come unless I wander the streets and sleep in alleyways, begging from passers-by. When I wrote my novel before last, *The Sa'd District's Residents Under Occupation*, I stole a wallet from the pocket of a livestock dealer in the working-class market called Miswak and spent an entire month in jail, where I finished the text. Read that novel, veteran of stabs, and see the depth of this experience.'

No doubt this was all madness, madness that heightened the awed admiration of his audience. I felt peeved that I was no longer a security agent, because if I had written an excellent report about this and added some spice to it, that would have helped me gain a promotion or raise.

Was this eccentric writer actually telling the truth – or was it merely a joke he was using to enchant his besotted admirers and put a beginning writer off track? But could I call myself a beginning writer when even now I didn't know how to begin? I wanted to ask him the date of that incident, the name of the livestock dealer whose wallet he had stolen, and in which of the capital's miserable prisons he had served time. How could he have written anything when he must have shared his cell with other men who hadn't gone to jail for the experience? It didn't seem prudent, however, to ask these questions, especially not then.

A young man, who had an untidy beard, wore a woven palm frond hat that had slipped almost halfway down his face, and held two books, one of which was remarkably large and the other so slender it was almost a pupil's copybook, asked: 'For *Eva Died in My Bed* – your brilliant, latest novel – what writing ritual did you employ?'

'A different ritual.'

Then the writer added, 'Very different, because I wrote it in the house of Ammuna al-Bayda', who is known to all of you. I rented her establishment, her ceremonies, and her zar sessions for two entire months while I produced the novel. I wrote with uncanny speed, which increased whenever I looked at the face of al-Bayda'. You certainly won't believe me, but this is what happened.'

In the home of Ammuna al-Bayda', the zar singer of Ethiopian heritage who enjoyed wide renown in our country? Crazy charismatics from all walks of life clustered around her! This man wasn't merely mad, he was a danger to writing itself, soiling it with such filthy locales: prisons, alleyways, and Satanic zar houses. If I sat there listening any longer, I would probably hear about a novel this luminary had written inside a public latrine. I looked at the green dial of my old West End watch, which I have worn for thirty years, and rose to leave, using as a pretext being late for a meeting. I would shut myself up in my room to think for a while. I might return another day – after I had armed myself with some insanity – to ask questions or listen some more. I was shuffling with my wooden leg as I moved away from that madness. Then I heard the voice of the luminary novelist call after me: 'Wait, veteran of stabs. I'll tell you about a novel I wrote in a public latrine reserved for conscripts while I was performing my military service. That's one of my best.'

*Chapter Three*

I was living in a small house near a stadium in a middle-class area of the capital. Despite all the pandemonium created by people frequenting the stadium – players, fans, and managers – especially when there was a decisive match between two of the major teams or a ceremony honouring a player who was retiring, I wasn't troubled by it. To the contrary: I would listen to the shouts and open my window, which had an unimpeded view of the field, and laugh delightedly at some of them while listening for any that blatantly threatened public security. I would even go over to the stadium, carrying my Parker pen, my yellow paper, and my list of suspects. Once, during a hotly contested game with lots of shouting and nail biting, I heard an agitated fan describe the player who missed the goal that would have guaranteed his team's victory as a traitor to the nation. The player's name was immediately etched in my mind and then written down on a paper I dispatched to my agency, but no one ever questioned him, and I was severely reprimanded for that report. The problem was that the fan had been referring to a team called

'The Nation', and the player who had dashed their hopes for victory was a member of that team.

The house consists of a single bedroom, which is painted grey, a cramped living room that has never been painted, a bathroom, and a small nook I use for a kitchen. Although I have few visitors, most of them former colleagues in the service or some of my few acquaintances, I take pains to ensure that my cramped living room is always spruce. It contains a number of leather chairs made in China, a table of high-grade teak, and two large vases of artificial roses. The supplies for my work – paper, implements, and weapons – used to be hidden in my room where no one could see them. My aunt, Th., was one of the few who had seen this gear. But once I had no further need for it, the agency sent a colleague to collect everything, leaving me just the paper, which I am definitely going to use to write the novel, because I've grown accustomed to its shape and feel. I consider these inspirational pieces of paper.

A.D., who was a huge fan of the team called 'al-Lablab',[2] which had held the top ranking among the teams for ages, and who was also a professional gravedigger in the Umran Cemetery, which is on the outskirts of the capital, accosted me at the door of my house. He had recently been honoured at the behest of the country's president, described as a patriotic citizen who deserves recognition. He was dressed in a green outfit like those worn by members of the Sufi

---

[2] The Arabic name of the hyacinth bean.

fraternal orders, and a long string of prayer beads made from hyacinth beans hung from his neck. On his left wrist he wore one of those metal bracelets that people think will cure rheumatism and that consequently are common in the country. He asked me whether I had seen the ceremony honouring him and the photos of him with the president. I hadn't seen any of that. So he asked me if I wanted to see the pictures, and I said no. I sensed he felt let down. As he left me, heading towards the stadium, I noticed a folded newspaper sticking out of his pocket. It must have contained some of those photographs. I thought he certainly had potential as a character in a novel and resolved to put him in mine when I wrote it. But what should the novel be about? How will I get started on it? Will A.D. appear in it as a cheerleader or a gravedigger? Or both?

Suddenly I noticed that my Aunt Th. – even though she was obese and over sixty – was running down a side street towards me. I felt apprehensive. I hadn't seen her for more than a month – that was when I had visited her for the Eid al-Adha holiday. Back then I had noticed a large number of satellite dishes on the roof of her house. I later learned that they belonged to a communications firm that used them as relays for their signals. They paid rent to my aunt for the use of her roof for this installation. Her husband, al-Mudallik,[3] told me proudly that influential people had interceded for him and that the contract wasn't merely a lucky break.

---

[3] Literally: 'the masseur'.

My aunt stopped in front of me, panting. Between gasps, she begged, 'Help, Abdullah . . . I beg you, help me. My husband has passed out. He suddenly collapsed in the living room at home. I don't know what happened.'

She had definitely ruined my day and driven away the many thoughts I had gained by sitting at the table of the luminary A.T. I had been going to devote myself to these as I started to plot out the novel, but felt obligated to come to her aid. I'll never forget – even though she disappeared for a long time when she claimed her back hurt – all the days she helped me until I was able to stand again. I found that I was dragging my wooden leg as I tried to run. I got it realigned once more with difficulty and made a point of stopping every few steps to feel the leg to make sure that it hadn't slipped again. When we finally reached my aunt's house, the situation had changed completely. We found her husband, the sports masseur, seated in the home's large living room, clad in cotton leisurewear made by the Egyptian firm Jil, delightedly smoking a local Bringi brand cigarette while watching a Twentieth Century Fox video starring the vintage American actress Ava Gardner on a television at the far end of the room. A slender girl was screaming from the summit of a crumbling mountain while a terrified lover threw her a rope. Having seen this video several times, I knew that the rope would break and that the movie star would fall into her lover's arms to provide a happy ending.

'What's the matter?' I screamed at him. I was a nervous

wreck. My throat was parched, my pulse elevated, and my good leg – the left one – was aching with pain.

Laughing, al-Mudallik replied, 'After a long wait, I've been offered a terrific part in the play *Perfumed Sealing Wax*, which will be presented soon at the National Theatre. I have the role of an elderly man who faints when he meets his beloved after a long separation. I was rehearsing the part. I succeeded brilliantly, didn't I?'

He was addressing my aunt while watching her out of the corner of his eye, and his smile revealed even more of his tobacco-stained teeth. Al-Mudallik had been in love with acting ever since his youth. He was intensely proud of his abilities but had never landed a role before, even though he had pursued theatrical troupes and pestered dramatists and directors. Eleven years earlier he had served several days in prison for disrupting a major theatrical show that had a star-studded cast. He had walked on stage carrying a wooden box, pretending to be a deaf man who shined shoes. So he chased the actors' shoes while communicating with sign language and grunts. This role was definitely not in the script. I saw my aunt move furiously towards the end of the living room. She returned with a broom that had a long, wooden handle. Al-Mudallik raised his hands to ward off the blow he sensed was about to fall. I slipped to the door before the violence, which was routine in my aunt's house, commenced. This violence would be short-lived, and their domestic harmony is long-lasting. Al-Mudallik loves my aunt madly, and she loves him madly too, although she would like him to give up smoking and to stop chasing after directors in the hope they will give him some idiotic part. I remember she once begged me to lock him up in one of our dark cells so she could get some relief from his face and antics. Then she returned tearfully to beg me not to. Al-Mudallik had been about to disappear forever, for I held a report that contained only two words, which I had written without feeling any compunction or guilt: 'Foreign Agent.'

Al-Mudallik would be a good character for a novel. That was obvious. If the luminary A.T. discovered him, he would definitely include al-Mudallik in a novel like the one about Eva. The title for this new novel would be: *The Failed Thespian*. I thought about this title again and decided it was a stupid, miserable title. The mental limitations of the woman who wore faded jeans or my own might be responsible – I have no imagination – but it was definitely not the fault of a great, luminary author like A.T. I will no doubt expand my imagination in the coming days and discover a title that fits the novel in which al-Mudallik, my aunt's husband, has a role. I was gradually slowing my pace on my way back home while observing the street's chaos: a number of teenage schoolboys had tied an emaciated dog to the trunk of a tree and were kicking it, and the only light pole in front of my house seemed to be tilting and in danger of falling over. Its wires touched each other from time to time, causing sparks.

I have two suits stored in the wardrobe in my bedroom. These were made to order for me a long time ago by the tailor Kh.R., who hails from the west of the country and who works as a tailor in front of a textile shop in the centre of the great market. One suit is navy blue and the other is made of grey velvet. I don't recall when I last wore a suit or what the occasion was. There aren't many occasions in my life that require me to look dapper. All the same, I took both suits out of the wardrobe and found that a thick spot of grease had dried on the blue one. I guessed I had worn it at a luncheon or dinner where I consumed greasy meat. The grey suit was spotless and gleaming, as though I hadn't worn it. I removed my clothes and tried it on, but it was too tight. I decided to take it back to Kh.R. to tell him to rip out the seams and resize it, now that I and my belly, which had long been slim, had expanded. I wished to practise A.T.'s rituals, one of which was wearing dapper attire when writing, whether he was in a swanky hotel or the departure lounge of an airport. Writing naked wouldn't be a problem for me nor would writing while homeless. Writing on a train, by the edge of a canal, or with the zar singer Ammuna al-Bayda' – none of those would be hard for me. I could rely on my long-standing friendships with prisons and prison wardens if I needed to spend months in prison writing my novel. I folded the suit and put it in a large shopping bag. I don't know how this bag made its way into my house, because I've never shopped for anything the size of this sack; I don't shop much. The bag must have been brought here by Aunt Th. when she came to feed me and wash my clothes until I could stand again.

I stopped in front of the tailor Kh.R. with the sack in my hand. He was busy eating a white-cheese sandwich, bits of which were splattering over the yellow shirt that dangled from his sewing machine, without him bothering to brush them off. He looked up at me but didn't smile. He put the sandwich on the shirt and stretched out a rough hand with scaly fingers. He shook my hand without rising. Formerly this tailor had left his machine to rush towards me the moment I came into view, greeting me with phrases reserved for the most important figures in the government. He had seemed keen to measure me with maximum accuracy. Frequently he would return the shirt or trousers, for which I had brought him the fabric, fully tailored and ironed even before I left the market. Occasionally he would decline my payment with strange insistence. I wouldn't, however, grumble about the loss of my job or my leg or brood about the cold hand extended by the tailor, who left his frigid palm in mine for only a moment, because I was on a mission to put in place the rituals that would allow me to write a novel. Now everyone knew that I had left the service, and I had reconciled myself to this. I opened the bag and handed him the suit, asking him to alter it to fit my new physique. He took it without any enthusiasm and placed it under his white plastic chair. Just as lethargically, he ran a measuring tape around my chest, waist, hips, and back, recording his readings on a dirty piece of paper, which had been balled up on the ground in front of him, and which he had picked up and smoothed out.

'Come back in ten days,' he said, his mouth spattering my suit with a mixture of saliva and cheese crumbs.

'Why ten days for a simple alteration that won't take more than an hour?'

'Who said an alteration is simple? That's harder than cutting out a new suit. Come back in ten days or take your suit and go to another tailor. I have a lot of work, Farfar.'

This was the first time he had used my nickname, which is employed only by colleagues in the service or those long-time friends who had either coined it or dated back to the time it was invented. It would be impossible to make this tailor work any faster. He returned to the cheese sandwich, toying with it, taking his time, chewing small morsels. The yellow shirt in his sewing machine was soiled by a thick spot of grease that I thought he might never be able to remove. I would return in ten days, which might become twenty days or an entire month. I would postpone the rituals of elegant writing and try writing naked or homeless instead. I think I've actually begun, because a passer-by has just paused in front of me, glanced at my wooden leg, and thrust his hand into his pocket to pull out a ten-piaster coin, which he stuffed into my hand. As he heads away, he repeats, 'Pray for me, Hajj. Pray for me, Pilgrim.'

*Chapter Four*

I was standing in front a bookstore called A'laf, which means 'fodder'. Owned by the Christian R.M., it is considered one of the oldest bookstores in the country. It is a fine trap for enemies of the state; we can arrest them there without any difficulty and without needing to chase them through the streets. I have always been puzzled by its name, which has never seemed a good one for a bookstore or even for a butcher's shop. R.M., a Catholic whose knowledge of Catholicism is limited to the denomination's name, has always offered the same response when asked about his bookstore's name. For the forty years since the bookstore opened, he has always said: 'Reading is fodder for the mind, folks – fodder for the mind, my friends. I don't mean that readers are like cattle but that books are like fodder.' In its perpetual search for strange and unusual subjects throughout this wide world, the Discovery Channel came to our country once, and the Christian R.M. appeared on one of its educational programmes. Surrounded by his books, he tried to explain in his broken English the name's meaning. The series' host, who seemed quite patient, rummaged through the books during the interview and asked about the latest type of fodder to arrive in his bookstore and about the most famous goat nourished by this provender. Even though the series went off the air subsequently, for a long time it survived in the store, playing on an ancient VCR connected to an equally ancient TV in a prominent corner of the bookstore.

This shop has two windows looking out on the public street in a crowded area downtown. In the windows, dozens of books are displayed, some the products of local authors and local publishing houses, and others imported from outside the country, whether legally or not. I saw cookbooks with covers portraying tables, overflowing with food, that bore no relationship to our dining tables. There were books on embroidery, bodybuilding, healing with charms and black caraway seeds, becoming a lawyer without studying law, and acquiring a waist like Naomi Campbell's in only two weeks without dieting. I noticed just one copy of a book that apparently was very popular, because placed beside it was a slip of paper on which was written 'last copy'. The title was *East, West, and Bust* and it was by someone I had never heard of. Truth be told, I'm not well enough versed in authors' names to know whether the person who wrote *East, West, and Bust* is famous or not. I decided to buy this book immediately and to try to read it all the way through, no matter what it was about, together with the novel *Eva Died in My Bed*, which I had come expressly to purchase. Perhaps the Christian would remember that he knew me from before and direct me to other books with which I could arm myself for the project I had undertaken – the project of writing a novel. *Eva* was not to be found, dead or alive, in either of the window displays, and I didn't find any other novel there. I knew there was a special rack for novels inside the bookstore, because in the past I had frequently dug through its contents, for professional reasons unrelated to reading or writing.

When I confidently entered the bookstore, a bareheaded teenage girl, who wore a black abaya with gold embroidery on its hem, was inquiring about the latest romance novels; a very slender young man was flipping through a book called *Liberation Movements Throughout the World: Their Pros and Cons*; and a middle-aged guy was clutching the book *Sex in Our Life* – a book of the type not displayed or purchased openly – and had his wallet out. The Christian R.M was hurrying back and forth between these three, opening his mouth to answer the teenage girl's request, preparing to receive the money for *Sex in Our Life*, and praising the book about liberation movements to encourage the slender youth to buy it. The sound of my wooden leg advancing across his newly mopped floor tiles, which smelled of Dettol, alerted him to my presence, and he swiftly pivoted. He appeared to feel pessimistic, vexed, or nervous, because he rapidly collected the money from the man purchasing the sex book, told the adolescent girl rudely that he didn't sell silly novels like those in his shop, and strode towards the slender youth to pluck the book from his hand. Then he picked up his keys from the table and looked at his ancient watch, which was a Jovial, as if planning to close the bookstore.

Intentionally not offering any word of greeting, I said slowly and confidently, 'Give me that last copy of *East, West, and Bust* and the novel *Eva Died in My Bed*, please.'

'Who died?' He raised his eyebrows in amazement.

'Eva died . . . Didn't you hear?' I replied even more confidently.

'What do you have against its author?' he asked in an abrasive or hostile tone he wouldn't have dared to use in the past. For quite a long time I had written him up for offences serious enough to land him in prison, closed his bookstore for days at a time, and impounded many books that he had counted on to turn a profit, but every time I came back I would find him smiling, energetic, and cheerful as he raced back and forth between his customers and the kettle in a corner of the store, so he could make Turkish coffee for me with just the right quantity of sugar. He might even give me tips on what to read or invite me to have lunch at his home. Once he gave me a book called *Magic and the Feats of Magicians* for my leisure reading. When the Discovery Channel televised him, he spoke at length in his broken English about how cooperative the local government was with him, and even declared that the police had never confiscated a single book from his racks. He was lying, of course.

'You know I'm no longer in the service,' I said, brushing aside his disparagement. I felt almost pitiful. I shouldn't have come to him in person now that I was retired and with that obscene leg. I should have sent him one of my colleagues who were still on the force and still ferreting out enemies of the state. They were people who could close both his bookstore and his mouth, which he was using to address me so impudently. But my colleagues themselves, unfortunately, were no longer actually colleagues and few sought me out. They would no longer even answer when my number appeared insistently on the screen of their mobile phones. When I occasionally remember my colleague A. B., who contracted a palsy and also lost his memory as a result of the traffic accident that injured both of us, and go to look in on him, I find his wife weeping, alone. She reports that everyone has fled from her husband, who had devoted his whole life to the service. He didn't even find anyone who would help when he needed a transfusion because of anaemia.

I won't grieve. I'll ask grief to take a hike so I can start my new project.

'Yes, yes . . . you're no longer in the service, I know, but employments like yours are parasites that don't die easily. I know many of your colleagues who have been out of the service for twenty years and still come and reach beneath my counter to defile the books. Why do you want *Eva*, Farfar?'

I was jolted again by his language and even more so by his use of my nickname, which is not intended for public use. He hadn't employed it even back when he had involuntarily become my putative friend.

I sensed that these successive jolts might drive me crazy or kill me or my desire to write the novel if I allowed them to get on my nerves. So I overlooked his hostility and requested the two books again, in a decisive tone this time, as I brought out my wallet and waved it in his face, which was that of a seventy-year-old with delicate features and a brown mole on the left side. R.M. walked to the window display where the book *East, West, and Bust* was located and opened it from the inside with a small key. He grabbed the book and locked the case again. Then he headed to a rack on which was written in shaky handwriting: 'Assorted Novels – Arab and Translated.' He extracted *Eva Died in My Bed* from the centre of the rack and placed the two books in a plastic bag on which was written in blue: 'Maktabat A'laf.' Then he handed me the bag and took from me a substantial sum of money. It was enough to make me wonder about those crazy readers who squander their cash on reading. I feared I was becoming one of them; all I possess is a pension from my former agency and a small amount of rent from a little house I inherited from my father. A family that had fled the west of the country, which was blazing with wars, lived there. Overcome by curiosity, I cast a glance at the rack of novels. They had attractive, coloured covers. For a moment I imagined my novel, which I will write, occupying its place in that rack soon . . . very soon.

I left the bookstore for the street, impatient to be home, because I was bearing one of the weapons of writing. I would break this weapon down deliberately and then go back to the Qasr al-Jummayz once I had finished. Then I would sit at A.T.'s table and discuss with him whether Eva had died on his bed or his hero's. I was confident that he would listen to me – arrogantly – and that the others would listen because he was. This time the girl in the faded jeans wouldn't be put off by my wooden leg and her heart wouldn't leap. She would come to accept my presence among them as if I were one of them. The teenager who had asked about romance novels was still loitering around the bookstore's window, scrutinising its contents book by book, her hand on her hip. An elderly man wearing a white shirt sporting the Mobil oil company logo was standing directly behind her, examining her more closely than the books and licking his lips. The slender youth who hadn't bought the book about liberation movements was standing across the street with a girl who was laughing audaciously and raising her hand from time to time to adjust her head covering, since a green silk scarf kept slipping off the top.

The sports fan and gravedigger A.D. was loitering between my house and the stadium this time too, but no match was scheduled to justify his presence. His newspaper was open in his hands, and he was looking at it and smiling enthusiastically. In his loud voice, which made him an excellent cheerleader, he called to a group of young men who were tussling with each other near him. He thrust the newspaper in their faces, ignoring their disgusted looks. I was afraid the honour he had unexpectedly received had driven him nuts. Since I didn't have time to check this out, I darted into my house and locked the door behind me, but no one knocked.

I took a seat on one of the leather chairs in my cramped living room after disconnecting my wooden leg from my body and placing it on my other chair. I opened the 'Fodder' bag and eagerly brought out the two books. *East, West, and Bust* was translated from English and consisted of vignettes that its American author had recorded on repeated trips around the world over the course of two years. (This was written on the back cover.) The cover blurb reminded the book's hypothetical reader that not all blows are delivered by a stick or a whip but that some are verbal. 'Dear reader, the language of this book will strike you mercilessly. So shield your mind carefully before you begin.' I didn't think too highly of this blurb and really didn't catch its drift. I reflected that I would never allow any comparable blurb on the cover of my book. Now I had the novel *Eva* in my hands. I looked through it giddily and gazed at the cover, which depicted a blonde girl with tousled hair, lying on a pink bed between a red heart and a knife blade. This was no doubt a symbolic portrayal of life and death, which A.T. had said lie on one bed beneath the same blanket. Only now did I understand his expressions that had seemed hard to understand when I heard them in the Qasr al-Jummayz. But my comprehension was still limited and doubtless I would attempt to master it more completely. It wasn't a big novel like those that make you turn directly to the last pages or to the middle, as I had heard some educated people say. It seemed very seductive reading that provided a portal to the world of writing. Perhaps I should push myself a little and devour it all in one go, as they say. I turned off my mobile phone and reached for my wooden leg to attach it to my body again. I went first to my landline and unplugged it and then headed to the comer I use as a kitchen, where I made a cup of hot tea to which I added a little mint. After taking a number of sips from it, I set the cup down before me and opened the book. I skimmed over the information and warnings on the copyright page and started directly with *Eva*, my current entry point for writing a novel. I began to read and ignored the unexpected knocking on the door and the voice of A.D. the sports fan, who was also a gravedigger, begging me to open up so I could see new photos, published in the day's papers, of the party honouring him.

*Chapter Five*

Friends, she's a bombshell.

Let me describe the bombshell for you and embellish her with the raiment of her enchantment. Let me display her for you on a sumptuous catwalk like the ones graced by Claudia Schiffer or the voluptuous maiden of Turkistan, Lena Parof.

I was in Moscow that year for the annual conference organised by the Cinema Academy there. They invite young directors from various parts of the world and even from our remote land, which isn't developed or known for its cinema. I was actually no stranger to Moscow – not some dazzled guest who searches for the right street and peers around gingerly. I had studied directing there, mastering the language and courting the women. I had sauntered down its back alleys and through its red and yellow squares. I had come to terms with its humour and seduction. Then I returned to my land, where I fell apart. There wasn't any film industry to employ me as a director, and there weren't even trifling parts for character actors. During those five years following my return I only produced a forgettable video about itinerant ice vendors during the summer season, casting for it a large number of my relatives and their friends. Lacking any acting experience, they roamed streets teeming with potholes and were excited about appearing in a film that was destined never to be shown and that lay in a desk drawer until it disintegrated. Even so, Moscow hadn't forgotten me and regularly invited me to attend the annual conference.

I was sitting in the lobby of the Aerostar Hotel, where we were staying. It was one of the city's venerable hotels. Built in Tsarist times, it had harboured combatants, prostitutes, and a few recent war profiteers who came to chat and relax. The structure had been renovated a number of times, and its reputation was rehabilitated too when it was added to the list of historic hotels. Now it welcomes cultural delegations from everywhere or football clubs participating in periodic athletic meets. When I was a student in Moscow, I frequented this hotel a lot and sat in its comfortable lobby watching a large, white pasteboard dove. It hung from the ceiling in front of the entrance and oscillated every time the door opened, as if to greet the new arrival. I would also welcome the perfumed and flushed smiles of female tourists from Europe or Asia; they were perhaps responding to my skin colour, which back then was uncommon in their lands.

I sat with the Mauritanian director Sidi Ould al-Binni, who had been my classmate. He had adopted modern ways in Moscow and returned home only to fall apart. Like me, he had regularly attended this annual conference, but his situation was better than mine, because a number of months earlier he had chanced to meet a French film crew who had come to plumb the depths of the Sahara and the world of desert men and women. They had hired him as an assistant to the director and thus refreshed his dreams to some extent. Ould al-Binni spoke non-stop about his French experience, explaining that he had produced a video for them that was entirely his own work from start to finish. It had revealed secrets they had never suspected: the untold truths about Saharan women's seditious charms and the men's virility – why rumps were plump and bosoms buxom. He had adapted the scenario, adding sweet songs interpreted by the vocalist Fatima Bint Lakkay and traditional dances performed by an ensemble of men and women dancing together.

'Was the video shown in France?' I asked. I was encouraging myself to hope that a similar film company would hear by chance of the cultural heritage of the Butana Arabs, who are camel herders in the centre of my country, or about the tribal dances of al-Mardum in the west, or might wish to preserve the cultural heritage of the south with all its uncouth savagery in a video to be shown in Europe, and that I would be an assistant to the director and the real creator of its segments.

'Not yet, no. But perhaps next month or at the latest in two months, and I'll attend the Paris showing,' he replied, his face radiant with happiness. His national costume, which consisted of an embroidered blue kaftan he wore over his grey suit, looked elegant if strange, and attracted attention in this distant setting.

Alexander Yahya was circulating around the area in his uniform, which consisted of red shirt and black trousers, carrying plates filled with food or empties and answering customers' complaints that the coffee was terrible or that the vodka tasted like rusty nails. He was a former ballet dancer and a veteran waiter in the Aerostar Hotel. I had long been puzzled by his name and wondered about the dissonance: how could an Alexander be the son of a Yahya or a Yahya be the father of an Alexander? The waiter, however, calmly relieved my curiosity. Apparently, he had frequently rehearsed his answer after being asked this repeatedly by the Arabs he met or the Russians themselves, of whom he was one. He was an Arab, like me, but knew nothing about the Arab world and had never seen the father who had planted his seed. His mother had told him that his father had studied dentistry and then returned to his homeland. His Caucasian features were attributable to his mother's genes and to the influence of the environment in which he lived. I was never convinced by his answer and continued to savour the thought that Alexander Yahya had an odd name.

Suddenly the bombshell appeared in the distance and approached very slowly.

She was a blonde whose ponytail was tied with a red ribbon and swayed when she walked. She wore a short, brilliantly coloured blouse that transformed her into a canvas at an exhibition of works by professional artists. Her leather sandals made no sound on the marble floor that echoed even a whisper. The very fact that her neck was unadorned made it an adornment, and because her hands were innocent of ornaments, they were themselves ornaments. Her features were such that if all women of the Earth shared them, the terms 'ugliness' and 'ugly' would vanish from all dictionaries everywhere. When she drew parallel to us – only to slip off down a corridor – a fascinating yet penetrating perfume was released by a flask . . . a human flask.

The Mauritanian Ould al-Binni grasped my hand, and I clutched his. He squeezed my fingers, and I squeezed back. We both suddenly stood up, staring down the corridor that had embraced her syncopated steps, and trembled. At that moment I regained enough awareness and resolve to free my hand from the Mauritanian and, trailing after the perfume, raced towards the first corridor only to find it empty. As I've said, I'm one of those who know Moscow very well and who have discovered dens of iniquity there unknown even to local residents. I recalled the face of Nathalie, the bronzed guitarist from Kiev. At least Nathalie was what was on her ID card, but I used to call her Natie. She liked that. She had wowed the audience with her face and the dexterity of her fingers at a public recital when she had refused to smile or sign any autographs for children or adults, not even for the organisers of the event. I had pierced the solid defensive wall she had erected by speaking to her of flying carpets and the lake of gold in the palace of Sultan Shahriyar while leaning stubbornly against the door of her hotel room. She became my compliant mistress who then lived with me for a number of months before she fled to America, which Russians referred to under their breath as 'the free country'. There she became one of the wildest opponents of communism, playing her guitar and singing lyrics she and other anti-communists composed. Then death discovered her in a cramped, walk-up apartment in Brooklyn. She was found by a member of the band she was performing with – shot dead by two bullets made in Russia. I wept when I heard about her death on the *Voice of America*, which regularly broadcast her songs to which I was addicted. I remember forgetting her some months after her murder and changing to a different radio station on a different wavelength. I recall living in lethal terror for a long time after she fled, fearful that I might be considered an opponent like her, whereas I was just an insignificant guest of a world far from my homeland, a guest who experienced a transitory pleasure and then sought out other ones.

I returned to my seat next to the Mauritanian director and found him singing a dance tune performed by Fatima Bint Lakkay, nodding his head ecstatically. His eyes were following a plump woman who was progressing down the middle of the lobby, shuffling her feet. Her appearance had obviously distracted him from the tremor he had experienced with me and returned him to his nation's culture, which was in his DNA. According to its standards, plumpness is not merely an enchanting feminine asset but enchantment personified.

'Have you seen that girl before?' I asked him in a shaky voice. 'I mean the one who passed us a short time ago.' I was hoping that he hadn't seen her previously, before she had appeared only to disappear, leaving us both pinned to our seats. I didn't want him to take precedence over me, not even in seeing a girl about whom I know only that she's a bombshell, who might glow for one day, or might continue to be a bombshell until she eventually fizzles out. Sidi Ould al-Binni wasn't listening to me. He was singing a tender stanza, which had become an embrace, from Bint Lakkay's song, and the plump woman on whom he was training his eyes stood now at the centre of the lobby. She was holding a large map before her face. She was looking for something on it – I guessed an ancient museum or the Monument to the Unknown Soldier in a city filled with museums, historic sites, and unknown soldiers. *She must be a tourist from Romania*, I told myself. She looked very Romanian and reminded me of an ophthalmologist who was the wife of a friend who had brought her back from Romania and settled her in my country.

'Have you seen her before?'

The Mauritanian stopped Bint Lakkay's affectionate song before the end, and his throat swelled with another song about a violet rose held by a lover who races with it towards his beloved. I saw him stand up, adjust his embroidered national kaftan carefully around his body, which was very tall and slender, and put on his gold-framed glasses. In seconds flat he reached a flower store that was one of a number of shops in the lobby selling things like souvenirs or tobacco products, or changing money. He emerged with a violet rose wrapped in cellophane and then presented it to the plump lady, whom I thought was Romanian. Then he headed for the exit with her. The map had fallen to the floor, but no hand picked it up.

Alexander Yahya walked slowly towards me after I had unsuccessfully tried to wave him down a number of times as he passed between tables. The tremor caused by the bombshell had only increased, and my eyes had fallen in love with the corridor taken by the blonde. *Come here, Alexander. Appear, Blonde.* In front of me was one of those silver curios that are frequently found on tables in hotels – I've never known why. I don't remember ever giving one a second look before, but I glanced at this one. It was a statue of a bull with eight horns and very wide eyes. Alexander polished it with a red towel and placed it before me.

'Who was that blonde girl,' I asked, 'who passed by here not too long ago, wearing a colourful blouse and leather sandals?' I was sure he had seen her and knew who she was. Alexander Yahya, as I well knew, is no ordinary waiter who moves between tables without noticing things; he possesses eyes like those of the bull he had placed before me. He had informed me once when we first became acquainted that he could sense the presence of beauty before he saw it. When he was a professional ballet dancer, before he became a waiter at the Aerostar, he had paused briefly to focus on the entrance to the theatre just at the moment when an enchanting woman entered.

'That's Eva,' he replied calmly. But I wasn't satisfied. The tremor hadn't died away. The sight of his huge Caucasian face and the hint of sarcasm that I sensed lurking in his eyes enraged me.

'Who is she, Alexander?'

'An employee in the hotel's public relations department; she only began working here two months ago. I don't know anything more about her.'

He left me quickly, heading to another table, where a man was becoming unruly because he had been waiting so long. I heard him swearing and cursing. I went back to the long corridor to stare at its emptiness. By the sheer intensity of my gaze I tried to force open one of the doors, which were clustered on the same side of the corridor, so that colourful Eva would emerge from it. An employee in public relations, she had begun work here two months ago; her syncopated step seemed an advanced degree in the fine art of relations. I don't know what came over me and why I was unable to control the tempest that stirred my emotions then. I was no longer the university student who lived in the country and succumbed to temptations. I was a normal guest who would spend a few pristine days with pristine cinematographers before walking off into the sunset, to wait for death or a sudden lucky break like the one experienced by the Mauritanian Ould al-Binni. When I have tried to relive that moment, my attempt to pinpoint it in my mind has failed – as did my urge to rush off to board the bus that would take us to the conference centre. I did see many of my fellow delegates who had spruced up for the occasion and were carrying small leather briefcases when they headed for the exit. I, however, was a guest of colourful Eva, and Ould al-Binni was a guest of the Romanian woman, who had revived his traditional culture in him and turned him into a tourist. I would strengthen my ties to the corridor and, if necessary, befriend it forcibly, knocking on every door until they all opened and Eva's face emerged from one of them.

I spent two hours seated in a pose I dubbed 'The Pose of Friends of Eva's Corridor.' I started to rise more than once, thinking I would knock on the doors to see who would respond, only to sit right back down. Two hours weren't a long time when devoted to the service of love. I had devised a hundred strategies I could use to win the heart of that colourful woman, but none seemed appropriate; Shahriyar, ruler of the thousand and one nights, was still a domineering sultan whom Shahrazad, with her power and self-confidence, was able to terrorise. There wasn't any magic carpet like those that had conveyed dreams in the age of legend to shorten the distance between the Nile and the Volga. I obviously had no reputation or influential and competently produced film to boast about to an employee of a public relations department. It could never have occurred to her that she had pierced a heart or conjured up a seduction when she crossed the lobby of the hotel where she worked. My one video, for which my family and the summer ice vendors had roamed the streets, had disintegrated, and I hadn't brought it with me. I considered it a memento and feared that it was lost, and the memory along with it.

Appear, Eva. Emerge from one of the doors, Eva.

*Chapter Six*

'Open up, Abdullah. Open the door, Farfar. I beg you.'

The voice of al-Mudallik, the husband of Aunt Th. had grown so loud I feared that the neighbours – even though they waste no love on me and grimace whenever they encounter me on the street – would think I was lying dead inside and rush to break down the door to discover my corpse. Al-Mudallik had begun to pound on the door and shout, calling to me, when I was close to the end of what was labelled 'Chapter One' of the novel *Eva Died in My Bed*, the first novel I had ever started to read. It held my attention even though I didn't understand much of its strange atmosphere and cryptic language, and even though its events took place in a country I knew nothing about. I was reading, feeling tense, shouting, 'You son of a bitch,' from one moment to the next while I continued reading – laughing occasionally at the conduct of the Mauritanian Ould al-Binni when he paid little attention to the beautiful blonde because he was dazzled by a plump woman, whom he stalked with a rose. I sensed the gap between writing and the profession I had followed for more than twenty years only to be rewarded with a wooden leg. The Russians had reached Nathalie in the land of freedoms, experiencing no difficulty in assassinating her, while many traitors escape our surveillance when they crowd onto a worn-out bus, slink away down winding alleys, or even hide behind their grandmothers' backs. I won't weep for the guitarist Nathalie (or Natie) as the hero of the novel did – he had a weak personality. I consider her a traitor to her nation; she sold it cheap and deserved what she got. If I had laid hands on her, I would have broken her neck. But what made me really tense was thinking about Eva even more than the novel's hero, whose name I didn't yet know. I'll call him M. M. for the time being until his actual name appears in what is left of the story, which I will definitely return to and finish after I open the door for al-Mudallik and see why he has come and started screaming in front of my house. The name M. M. has stuck in my memory even though it has been fifteen years since I shadowed the leftist who had these initials. Then he gave up politics to become – as he still is – a used-car dealer. M. M. was a cultured man who had studied some disastrous subject in Moscow and returned to cause us problems. Could this story be about him? I'll keep that in mind. Yes, once I finish this story I'll compare it to the true story of the former leftist. I'm no longer in the service, but its parasite is hard to eradicate, as the Christian bookstore owner pointed out.

I slowly attached my wooden leg and was in a foul

mood when I headed to the door. I kept turning to gaze back regretfully at *Eva*'s cover; I had left her at a gripping moment.

Al-Mudallik, my aunt's husband, was standing impatiently at the door, clad in a custom-made sweatsuit bearing the white-and-blue emblem of the Marid Football Club, for whom he had been a masseur for over forty years. Over his shoulder was slung an inexpensive dark black cloth bag, and he wore sports shoes without any laces. The sports fan, who also dug graves, was still out there, seated now on a distant rock, his newspaper spread before him, calling out to anyone who passed to come have a look. I was overcome by a strange feeling then that the sports fan was shadowing me. He might have chosen that seat to keep an eye on me. But why would he be tailing me? Doubtless this was a silly feeling, and I set it aside very quickly.

'What do you want?' I asked al-Mudallik, knowing full well from my investigative experience derived from years in the service that he had come to remind me of the opening of the play *Perfumed Sealing Wax* in which he had – after a long wait for any part in any play – landed the role of the old man who faints when he is finally reunited with his beloved. Back when I was still working, al-Mudallik had leaned on me for more momentous favours. Once he had wanted me to free a member of his team apprehended for taking dope in a house of ill repute, and another time someone he knew had bounced a cheque with a bicycle merchant. Then there was the time he wanted me to intercede with a neighbourhood businessman and get him to work with al-Mudallik and reschedule the amount he owed. One time he even asked me to travel with him for moral support to a provincial city in the country's east, which was where he was from, because he had heard its theatre troupe was looking for talented amateurs to perform in a non-professional theatre competition.

'Don't forget, Abdullah: the play opens in just two hours. Your aunt claims her lower back pain is too severe for her to attend. I'm counting on you to support a family member. A star will be born in your family tonight.'

He held his head high, arrogantly, there was a confident look in his eyes, his lips were provocatively pursed, and he made the tin medal on his broad chest sway by touching it from time to time.

I wasn't really convinced that a star would be born in our family, if only because he had long since passed the age at which stars are born. No part as a man who passes out for a number of minutes immediately before the curtain closes would ever make him a star. But I wouldn't disappoint him. I would put off reading the story until another time and go to see the play. Being polite didn't come naturally to me. In fact the suppression of polite behaviour formed part of my intensive training when I first began my career, but a person's nature can change. My departure from the service may cancel out its fundamentals.

'Are you going to perform in your sweats?'

'Of course.' He laughed elatedly. 'These clothes, Farfar,

are essential: the old guy who faints is a former athlete. Even though that's not mentioned in the play, the audience will grasp this from his clothes. This is what they call inspiration. Got that? Enter by the side door of the theatre, and I'll get you a seat in the premium orchestra section, but don't be late.'

He rapped my shoulder repeatedly, and his hand felt like dry firewood. I don't know why I almost trembled, because his taps didn't hurt. This word 'inspiration' was very beautiful. It was a new word for my dictionary – like the word 'rituals'. I'll use it at the Qasr al-Jummayz and dazzle the luminary A.T., the girl in faded jeans, and everyone else who sits at that refined table. Once I become a great writer, I'll frequently discuss inspiration and its role in writing.

My old West End watch said it was 5 p.m.; al-Mudallik lifted his hand to hail a three-wheeled, motorised rickshaw. They are used here because the traffic is so heavy. This one was green, and its roof was brown fabric. I heard the driver yell, 'Welcome, Captain. Hop in, Captain.' Al-Mudallik squeezed himself into it. His hand, which was extended towards me, traced the hour of the drama's opening in the air.

I left the door of my house ajar and headed towards the cheerleader who was also a gravedigger. He was seated on that distant rock with his newspaper in front of him. I sat down beside him and saw that his eyes looked blank – as if he were in a daze. I wanted to humour him a little and gazed at several photos that portrayed him clothed in green Sufi garb with a string of lablab bean prayer beads around his neck as he dug a grave; in gleaming white raiment greeting the country's president when our head of state girded him with a medal; surrounded by family members, friends and members of the Lablab Club team, with his medal dangling down his chest. I said, 'Your pictures are beautiful, very beautiful,' but that didn't revive him.

He responded, 'That's not all of them.' Then he rose, leaving his newspaper where it lay on the ground. He moved away and disappeared down an alley. His faint voice hadn't been that of a great cheerleader, and he walked like a man lost in the desert, turning right and then left. I gathered his paper from the ground, took it with me, thinking he might return to look for it, and entered my house.

The National Theatre, where the play was being performed, was relatively far from my house, and my damn wooden leg couldn't cover that distance without coming loose or falling off. I tried to stop a number of vehicles that passed nearby, but the drivers either didn't turn to look or turned and looked back without wanting to stop. I finally found a motorised rickshaw like the one al-Mudallik had taken and reached the theatre only when the show was about to start. I found him scowling and waiting for me at the side door. He led me silently to my red velvet seat in the front row, lifted the folded newspaper from it, seated me, and slipped off to race backstage. I was surprised to find the novelist A.T. sitting there in the orchestra section. The girl with faded jeans was next to him and leaned towards him from time to time to whisper some comment to him. I was close enough to hear what she said. She was actually asking whether he had read any of her novel, *A Moment of Love*. The novelist didn't reply, but I noticed that his nostrils were flared and imagined that he was enjoying the perfume that must be wafting from that dotty girl. I tried to compare her to Eva, but found no similarity. I wouldn't greet the novelist at this stage in my efforts and would avoid his glances if he chanced to look my way. I had a lot of work ahead of me before I joined his table, and by then I would be the sole star there.

The show got off to a rousing start. A group of people carried in a man's body and placed it on the stage. From the dialogue it became clear that he was a drowning victim they had pulled from the river and that they were trying to identify him. A man sitting beside me whispered to me that the drowned man symbolised the nation, and the people hauling the corpse from the river were citizens who discovered that their nation was drowning. I scrutinised the man's features so I would remember him when I investigated his ideas later. I was beginning to dig through my pockets for a piece of paper when I recalled that I was no longer in the service and that I no longer carried around pieces of yellow paper in my pockets. *The worm of our service isn't easily exterminated! What a trivial worm it is!* The show continued for an hour until it was time for al-Mudallik to appear during the second act, which ended with him passing out. Then the play would continue with the remaining acts.

A woman appeared first, walking slowly and repeating the line, 'It's impossible . . . impossible.' Then al-Mudallik appeared from the other side, wearing his same sweats. He was walking heavily, leaning on an ebony stick. I saw him approach the woman, shouting, 'Halima, beautiful Halima!' The woman screamed, 'Nu'man! My handsome Nu'man! Impossible.' At that moment al-Mudallik fell, landing on his back on the wood of the old stage and making a dreadful sound. Everyone in the audience applauded, and the curtain closed.

At first I assumed that I had concluded my mission – watching my aunt's husband in the role that he believed would make him a star. I considered leaving so I could continue reading about Eva and learn how her relationship with the story's hero developed. But al-Mudallik would certainly search for me at the end of the show. If I left now, he would accuse me of having decamped before I witnessed his performance. So I sat still, waiting for the end. Then the novelist A.T. and his companion brushed past me, without giving me a glance, as they headed for the exit.

It took longer than usual for the next act to begin, as I knew from shadowing suspects who entered theatres and from following them inside. I heard members of the audience murmur or whistle in annoyance, and some started to leave, one at a time.

When the curtain finally opened, a middle-aged man, clad in a tunic and turban, appeared on stage holding a microphone. He said, 'We regret to announce to our distinguished audience that a cast member has unexpectedly fallen ill. So the rest of the performance will be cancelled today. Please retain your ticket stubs and present them tomorrow, if you will. Thank you all for attending our show.'

Then the curtain closed again.

When, exhausted and fearful from hearing that al-Mudallik hadn't regained consciousness, my aunt – whom I had roused from her back pain and brought with me weeping – and I reached the hospital to which he had been taken, the physician told us that they had discovered the sedative Ativan in his blood – a small amount, but enough to kill a man his age who suffered from high blood pressure and hardening of the arteries. He had apparently wanted to pass out for real when he fell on stage and not merely faint like an actor – to ensure that his name would be etched in spectators' minds not as someone who had played his part well, but as someone who had actually lived it. In his bag, which they had opened, instead of the suicide note they expected, they had discovered thousands of pieces of pink paper cut to resemble hearts. Inscribed on these in very firm handwriting was the single sentence, 'I thank you for your admiration and sign this with my love.'

This ordeal didn't kill al-Mudallik, although the doctors expected it would. I read their pessimism clearly on their faces when they injected his arm, which was as dry as a stick of firewood, with both clear and coloured solutions. After he regained consciousness, he told us he hadn't wanted to die and then asked for a Dunhill cigar, even though these were virtually impossible to find in this country. He distributed the pink paper hearts himself – after adding to each the name of the person receiving it – to the hundreds of people who flocked to the hospital or his house once he returned there; my aunt slaughtered two plump lambs.

Al-Mudallik, who no doubt was insane, would make a unique character for a novel, as I remarked during the days when he became my sole preoccupation, robbing me of my new enjoyment: reading the story of Eva. I brooded dozens of times about making him the central figure of my novel, which I shall write but fear someone else may write, especially one of those visitors who came to see him in the hospital during his convalescence – people who weren't his acquaintances or friends or even appreciative fans of an actor who had actually fainted on stage. I took time to inspect the faces of these folks, relying on my investigative experience. I imagined repeatedly that they were amateur writers in search of a text to write. I believe the effort I invested during that period when I consoled my weeping aunt, standing vigil with her night and day, qualifies me for first dibs on al-Mudallik as a character. I'm not about to allow anyone to steal this character from me.

I was lying on my tummy in bed, my wooden leg within

reach and Eva with her beautiful cover in my hand. The night was young. I could hear the intermittent noise of vehicles speeding past, and through the open window, that spring night, came the delightful smell of roasting meat.
*I want to begin reading now. The second chapter seems to be calling out to me: 'Read me, Farfar. Read me . . .'*

*Chapter Seven*

Does that make sense, Alexander Yahya? Does it compute? To leave my ear stinging like this and not bring me a matchstick to scratch it? You're still hovering around the tables indefatigably, bearing your huge Caucasian face as you pretend to be affectionate at times and occasionally even more than affectionate. That Mexican provokes you by sitting indecorously with his right leg propped on a chair and by puffing the smoke from his Havana cigar in your face, which becomes littered with the ashes of his delight. Why don't you back away?

The hotel lobby had suddenly filled from one end to the other as the huge dove at the portal bowed to greet dozens of new visitors. They were a mixed bag of Europeans, Asians, Americans, and others whose features I was unable to place. The Japanese among them behaved like enthusiastic robots designed especially for tourism in this country. Their cameras and mobile phones were weird; and their facial features were actually identical. For a while I watched the dove bow, thinking that it might welcome the Mauritanian Ould al-Binni and his plump Romanian, but that didn't happen. I returned my gaze to Eva's corridor to contemplate its emptiness, but Alexander still hadn't brought me a matchstick to scratch my ear. Why did I ever quit smoking? I would have been able to lay my hands on a matchstick if I still smoked.

Then one of the Japanese women approached me; she was devoid of charm and allure. With her robotic features appropriately emblazoned on her visage, and the tight denim shirt, which she wore the American way – buttoned tightly around her chest – this woman didn't appear to be a life raft that would rescue me from Eva's empty corridor. At first she addressed me in the language of the Toyota, Mazda, and Nissan, but I continued to shake my head to show that I didn't understand. Then she returned and managed a few words of tentative English. I gathered that she wanted to drag an empty chair from my table to add to her companions' crowded one. She apparently changed her mind, however, and I suddenly found a flaming robot seated near me, on the chair that the Mauritanian had abandoned when he rushed off with the violet rose, after the Romanian woman had reunited him with his homeland's cultural heritage. I didn't want a mechanical companion like this. I had to listen as she asked a question or two about my identity, my nationality, and my business in a country that had shed some of its influence and lost its prestige after nurturing Gorbachev and allowing him to experiment with perestroika. I answered that I was an ordinary tourist, taking snapshots of the Kremlin,

Red Square, and the fortresses of wolves scattered here and there. I didn't say I was involved in cinema for fear her questions would inevitably branch out and lead her to discover that since I left the Cinema Institute my only significant productions had been bowel movements, and that I'm not especially cultured. I haven't, for example, read any Japanese literature yet and only heard by accident of Yukio Mishima, the great Japanese novelist who wrote *Confessions of a Mask*, at one of the conference sessions. The Japanese woman laughed profoundly – I didn't know why – and plucked from her handbag, which was made of hippo skin, an embroidered handkerchief to wipe away her viscous tears. Her robotic face turned red then, and I must have blushed too. I looked around nervously to search for anything funny enough to have made this automaton laugh, since my reply wasn't supposed to warrant laughter on this scale. I saw seated directly behind me a man who resembled a young Fidel Castro. Facing the Japanese woman, he spread his right hand over his lips and threw her a kiss. Now the Mauritanian's chair was vacated once more and the empty one next to Castro – this lover of automata – was filled.

Finally, colourful Eva appeared. I was perplexed when I saw the corridor fill suddenly with her languorous, syncopated gait. I popped to my feet just the way a pupil sitting at a street corner does when he sees his teacher walk past. I was the schoolboy and my teacher didn't have a moustache, walking stick, or resonant voice, but instead every grace. I now blocked her progress, after she had taken a number of steps, by deliberately dropping my wallet in front of her, pretending it had slipped out of my pocket accidentally. I knew that this was an old trick for starting a conversation with a stranger and expected the colourful woman to realise that it was merely a ruse and walk on by. Cute girls learn fast and grow accustomed to unmasking tricky strategies even as young teenagers. I remember that dozens of items would be dropped in front of Tumadir, my neighbours' daughter, when she walked down the street, and she wouldn't pick up a single one.

Eva certainly surprised me when she leaned over and we picked up the wallet together. For a moment our fingers touched. She grasped the wallet, handed it to me sealed with a smile, and then headed for the elevator. I seized hold of a speck and set about transforming it into a bushel that I could carry back to my seat in the first instance, next to my room when I retired there early in the evening to bathe and change clothes, and then on to a meeting with the Mauritanian Ould al-Binni when I discovered him reclining in a leather armchair at ten, holding a menu open to European Favourites. The fragrance of his skin had nothing to do with the desert then. He had changed into a tourist and was preparing for a night on the town with his plump female tourist. Film crews that might turn up to document the desert in trifling ways no longer interested him.

'Do you think a smile's enough?' he asked without

looking at my face. His eyes, instead, were cruising around the restaurant. They were the eyes of an expectant man waiting impatiently, not those of a comrade listening to his pal.

'That's enough for now. She could have ignored the whole thing and walked by if I hadn't appealed to her. I'll tease other smiles from her . . . even laughs. I'll marry her, Ould al-Binni – you'll see.'

I was all wound up and ready to explode. I pulled the menu from his hand and opened it to Russian Favourites. His entire face became a smile. I heard him say very softly in Russian, 'I'll pay for your honeymoon – any place you choose.'

He had risen to join his Romanian tourist, who had appeared in the distance wearing green velvet trousers and a sleeveless yellow blouse that made her look even plumper than she did in the morning. The Mauritanian must have extolled her plumpness extravagantly during his excursion with her. He may have briefed her on his country's culture and admitted her to it. *I'll eat a Russian dinner alone tonight. But that's all right, because before long I'll be dining in female company, I'm sure of that. The conference ends in three days, and I'm supposed to depart then for the land of thirst, unemployment, and miserable grovellers waiting for any miracle. But I won't leave. I'll find some way to stay on and finish what I have begun.* Just yesterday when I had told Alexander Yahya about my failure in the movie business back home, and about the lack of any desire on the part of the Russians to offer me a job, even though I've attended their conference for five years and know many of their actors and directors, he had made me a piddling proposal, claiming that he would find employment for me in one of the bureaus that do translations into Russian. This was an agency owned by one of his relatives, a woman named Sansha, who wouldn't turn down his request. The firm specialised in translating biographies of leaders, documents relative to the wars that flare up everywhere, and novels that create a buzz in the Third World. I would doubtless be a good fit for them. 'Sansha is a very cultured and compassionate person – you'll like her.'

When he said this, his Caucasian eyes widened and then contracted, and his hands jerked in an alarming way. So I found myself rejecting his proposition without giving it a second thought. I wouldn't translate a leader's biography filled with obsequious comments that he had penned or that more likely had been ghostwritten for him without the least regard for truth or emotions; I wouldn't translate documents detailing atrocities that interested only their victims; I didn't think I would succeed in translating a novel, because I consider the translation of literature to be an act of betrayal of its truth. All forms of literature should be read in the original language. Alexander paid little attention to my reaction and didn't withdraw his proposal – my brusqueness and boorishness notwithstanding. He left it open and resumed his routine of hovering among the tables. Now I found myself flirting with that proposal, offering it a rose and a kiss. I left my seat before I had finished my dinner and headed to the hotel's lobby in search of the Caucasian waiter but failed to find him. He had finished his shift and left for the evening.

I spent a third of this slow and arid night on Pushkin Street gazing at the barber shops that were scattered here and there. Now that they had begun to offer really short cuts like those of American Marines, the shops were packed with young men. I gazed at the huge posters for the ballet *When the Moon is Full* and for a TV series *The Master and Margarita*, which was based on a novel by Bulgakov, or sat in the corner of a crowded coffeehouse, thinking of a hundred strategies to introduce the enchanting Eva to my life. The deeper I plunged into my thoughts, the more resolute I grew. When I left the street, heading back to my hotel, and observed the Cuban who looked like a young Castro staggering along with his friend the Japanese robot, I decided that I should besiege Eva's heart directly by accosting her in the morning in the guise of a crazed lover, and request space there. She would definitely spurn me, but I wouldn't give up. Great victories, as I knew, came only after dozens of attempts. I knew I wouldn't sleep that night and that if I dozed off, my slumber would be a restless nap. So I changed course and entered one of the city's large bookstores that cater to the literary set. I wanted a page-turner that would rouse me even more and keep me company through the remainder of the night, like a beloved in her lover's embrace. The young clerk in the bookstore recommended a novel by Mark Zakharov, saying, 'You won't fall asleep until you've finished it.' I needed that advice.

The dove greeted me with her colourful beak as I entered. The lobby was almost empty. The tourists had apparently scattered to every area of the city, where dozens of festivals are held every year. Lovers of history come to watch history unfold. Lovers of opera come to spend the evening in Moscow's Art Theatre. Even lovers of the culinary arts come to taste the exotic dishes of diverse peoples in the annual food festival. The Mauritanian was sitting there despondently, without a companion, looking morose. I grasped that the Romanian woman had dumped him as swiftly as she had initially befriended him. 'Can you imagine that I wasted expensive perfume – Coco Chanel! – for which I spent a hundred roubles? She said I was uncivilised, but I was exceptionally civil with her. I never spat on the ground. I wasn't baffled by the baffling streets. I didn't sing any of Bint Lakkay's songs, because I thought she might consider that backward, and so forth and so on. She even moved; she got her bags and left for another hotel.'

He spoke so cholerically that I almost laughed, but my own tension that I had suffered since morning prevented me. I consoled him, not knowing whether that would help him shake off his gloom. 'Don't be downhearted, my friend. She'll return to you faster than you think, because you're the only one who will give her a second look now that plumpness no longer turns heads.'

I stretched out on my bed in my room on the fourth floor with the novel by Zakharov in my hands. I read it by the faint light of the reading lamp, which was placed beside the bed. The novel was a page-turner from the get-go. It was set in eighteenth-century Russia, and the heroine was a poor village girl named Zareba. She was sold to a one-eyed, crippled slave dealer, who toured the villages displaying his wares. Her paternal uncle, in whose house she lived after her father died and her mother married another man, sold her to him. During her first night in the arms of the merchant, she fought him off ferociously, using her nails and teeth, even though she felt dizzy, but didn't escape from his clutches. She became the hundredth victim of a man who bought poor girls and enjoyed them savagely for a certain number of nights. Then he turned them into servants. They enhanced his prestige and travelled with him so he could sell them to village women.

I was kept awake by travelling with Zareba, and her destiny among all those other women condemned to the same fate saddened me. I don't know when I dozed off; when I awoke suddenly, I found the book open on my chest. The reading lamp was still on, and morning's intense light was visible behind the window curtain. The clock mounted on the wall indicated that it was now 9 a.m. That was late, and the colourful Eva must have passed down her corridor early that morning. That didn't matter. I would spruce up at once and surprise her in one of those rooms; her office must be there. Alexander

Yahya must be there too, and I could accept his proposal and work as a translator of fraudulent biographies, documents spawned by atrocities, and cheesy novels that had created a buzz in the Third World.

*Chapter Eight*

The worn green dial of my old West End watch indicated that it was twelve noon – the time the novelist A.T. was most frequently seated amidst both admirers and critics at his favourite table in the Qasr al-Jummayz coffeehouse. I was present too, but didn't know whether I had come as an admirer or critic of the work I had read.

Today, at dawn to be precise, at the hour when traffic starts to flood the streets and all noises blur together, I finished the novel about Eva. I had polished off the remaining chapters in one go and felt giddy. Yes, I felt giddy despite all the troubles I had faced in reading the work. I had sensed I was scaling a dreadful mountain without being allowed to lag behind or pause to catch my breath. My mind had actually climbed that mountain, and I had learned that there are other things to enjoy in life over and above scrutinising roads and faces when on patrol, writing police reports on yellow paper, and standing deliriously at a reception given to honour you for uncovering a secret. I was astonished to find that the idea of writing a novel that had led me to this road hadn't deserted me once I read a real novel; to the contrary, the idea had become more entrenched. *I'll start writing right away and offer what I've written to the novelist at his gathering and to other novelists, readers, and the whole world when my book is published. Moreover, I'll read other books I obtain from the Christian R.M. and from all the other bookstores in the capital. I'll read and read.* I began to repeat this while recalling Eva's novel and all its events, exactly as if recalling a sweet taste I had enjoyed and didn't want to relinquish. The novel's hero, whose name is never mentioned although I thought of him as M.M. after the leftist used-car dealer, actually began to pursue the colourful blonde – 'colourful Eva', as he referred to her through all the pages of the novel – but she kept on rejecting him. He grew addicted to her brutal love, as he said, and she became addicted to tormenting him. In the Aerostar Hotel, where many of the events transpired, she scratched his face repeatedly with her fingernails, which she deliberately allowed to grow longer to hurt him. She gave him a Russian band's recording of a song called 'Bug off, please!' and incited some of her friends to hunt him down on a desolate night and choke him, but still he wouldn't leave her. Thanks to Alexander Yahya, whom he referred to as 'the Caucasian with the weird name', he obtained that position in the translation bureau with Sansha Marov, who was the exact opposite of Eva. She was delicate, easy-going, and had black hair. She paid him an advance for several months of his salary and set him to work straightaway translating an Arabic book that was reminiscent of works of the Arab cultural heritage: *The Touch of Silk in the Language of Ewers* by an author he had never heard of. He didn't feel well grounded in the Arab cultural heritage but began the translation despite his obsessive love for Eva, whom he pursued whenever he could. Next came the events that perplexed me and forced my mind, which was new to reading, to pause repeatedly to highlight or reread a sentence that had perhaps escaped me or that seemed counterintuitive. Sansha, who was a thirty-one-year-old widow, lived in a comfortable house, as the author said when describing it:

> Her house was a haven of violets and gardenia bushes, of morning rays of sunshine following pitch-black nights, and also of an intoxication that in some mysterious way she expertly induced; beneath her rose-coloured blouse, she had a scar on her chest from an old wound, the wound of her love and its loss.

At first the hero lived in a small room that opened out on the courtyard of Sansha's house. At this time he was trying to reconnect with the Moscow he had lived in for a long time, back when he had mastered its language and seduction. He had left Moscow and chased after the mirage of his dreams – to become a renowned cinematographer in his own country. He had returned to Moscow as a visitor each year for the cinema conference but had never screened anything; this visit felt different:

At first Eva seemed a sweet basil blossom that forced me to inhale its perfume. Now she appears to be a bitter colocynth roasted to perfection and served to me at the table of a five-star restaurant. I did not possess Moses' staff to drive away lust's beasts, and the staff of my fallibility wasn't a snake that would coil up after devouring the magic of Shahrazad decked out in a hundred captivating robes. From her face I derived insanity, and from my disfigured visage she derived the ability to drive me crazy.

Sansha slipped into his room one night:

She was anointed with a mute demon that fought with me silently, knowing that I lacked any ammunition. She wore a diaphanous green nightgown that didn't merely direct my gaze to a widow's hungry body but fully disclosed it to my eyes. I discerned her seductive charm and trembled. I didn't know what drew her to my despair and cigarettes, which I had resumed smoking non-stop, when I considered her only as a means of obtaining residency so I could reside near the colourful predator.

The hero resisted Sansha's charm that and many other nights without making her feel that he was avoiding her, because he didn't want to lose his menial job. Using as a pretext his preoccupation with translating the cultural heritage book, he moved to a small room on the roof of one of the buildings, but Sansha continued to slip in there to visit him many nights, alleging that she wanted to ask him about the translation. The very night that Eva stopped spurning him and yielded to his insane passion, he stopped spurning Sansha and fell into her arms:

> That night the colourful woman smiled at me, in fact laughed profoundly, and I saw that her entire body was laughing. She didn't call me crazy, or worthless, or African, or claim I had defective genes as she had in the past. Her fingernails were trimmed and tinted violet; these weren't nails for scratching but for loving. She led me to her house, which was very humble and located in a poor neighbourhood filled with tobacconists, glaziers, and the voices of old women and girls. She was holding my hand, and I didn't feel hungry or thirsty. I stood in front of her house for some moments staring at the door's rusty hinges and termite-infested wood, and at a scrawny brown cat that was weaving about. Even before I entered, the door squeaked as it opened, disclosing a small living room with a painting hung opposite the door. When I left Eva, whom I had pursued for more than three months, her wide-open eyes gazed at me apprehensively; I sped to Sansha. I had no idea how she had suddenly become embedded in me like an eraser that wiped away all traces of my passion and folly. Sansha was with me now in an inviting room rich with legends inside a home perfumed intoxicatingly by violets, on a bed with rose-coloured sheets and pillowcases. Her nightgown was diaphanous and green, and her body was totally alive. Eva died that day, and Sansha sprang to life.

I didn't understand the meaning of the ending at all and attributed my confusion to a lack of experience with reading. It must be a really great ending from the perspective of people who read a lot – 'writing by the jinn', as the woman who wore faded jeans had said. I had identified with the writer from the beginning, racing along with him in his pursuit of Eva, being wounded when her rough fingernails scratched him, and choking when he was nearly strangled. I was enraged in equal measure with Sansha when she tried to leverage the job she had given him to win his affections. But now, the ending had me perplexed; it perplexed me a lot but also intoxicated me at the same time. *I have finally read a novel; tomorrow I will write one.*

As far as the Mauritanian Ould al-Binni is concerned, his Romanian tourist had returned to the hotel again in search of him, as the hero had expected, and he travelled with her to Europe. That was his last appearance in the novel, although the waiter Alexander Yahya, who remained in the story to the final chapter, mentioned him from time to time.

The Qasr al-Jummayz was awash with its brand of controlled anarchy, and its Ethiopian waitresses tripped harmoniously back and forth. A number of individuals with the facial scars of marginal tribes from the east of the country were whispering in a corner, and an elderly partisan – one of those no longer considered threats by our security agencies – had buried his face in a newspaper with a bold headline in red that screamed: 'Nation in Danger.'

Who said the nation was in danger? Who had given that newspaper permission to print a bold headline like that? Even though I had retired, I was confident that my colleagues still in the service would be able to nip any danger in the bud. I was conjecturing, without really knowing, what special danger the bold headline referred to. I reflected some more – it might be the danger of a flood or famine or the sugar cane flu that I had heard you could contract by chewing sugar cane.

A.T. was not at his usual table. I saw the girl who wore jeans sitting all alone there. Her pink headscarf had slipped from her small head, revealing hair tinted a brown that didn't suit a local girl. I approached her, trying to keep my vile leg from making a sound on the pockmarked tile floor. But the girl must have heard, because she raised her head as I started to sit down on a chair a Goldilocks distance from her.

'Shukrallah?' she asked as she looked down at my damn leg. 'Isn't that right?'

I felt the wood twitch and sensed that I stood out like a sore thumb in this place. I wondered why she had come up with the name Shukrallah in particular just then.

'Abdullah Harfash . . . Abdullah Farfar.'

'Right. Sorry. You came once and then disappeared.'

She turned her eyes from me and opened her leather handbag, which was scuffed at the edges. She took out a small mirror and held it in front of her pimply face, which she contemplated absent-mindedly. Inside her handbag I was able to spot a tube of pink lipstick, violet nail polish, and a small packet of Chiclets that had been opened: two had been removed. She didn't seem keen on engaging in any type of conversation. Although I sensed she was still apprehensive about me, I needed to know where the novelist was.

'Where's the Master today?'

'They got him,' she replied sourly and put the mirror back in her bag. She closed it and stood up, not forgetting to glance briefly at my vile leg.

'Who got him?'

'Who do you think? Two idiots from those inane agencies.'

She certainly upset me when she called my two honourable colleagues, who had been acting in the line of duty, 'idiots' and described the nation's watchful eyes that safeguard its security as 'inane'. She was an impetuous girl who would trample on a beehive knowing full well what was in it. Now she had put her foot into a hornet's nest without realising it. Even if she had known, she would have considered it an old nest. I quickly suppressed my agitation and caught her while she was putting the strap of her handbag over her shoulder before she could move away. The remaining pimples on her face looked ebony black in the sunlight falling on her face through the coffeehouse's window.

'Where did they take him?'

'I don't know. Who knows where they take people?'
'What did he do?'

She didn't answer my last question because she had already left. I looked around, anxiously searching for anyone who had been at the novelist's table during my one previous visit: the slender youth who held two books and asked about the plot idea for the *Eva* novel, the girl in a violet tunic who spread her knees and didn't close them, the old man who smoked quietly while his hands shook, and the journalist known for his fabricated dialogues. There was no one present I could ask, so I rose from my seat in frustration. I still retained Eva's taste in my mouth and wanted to dazzle the novelist with it when he learned that I had read him, even if my level of reading was still rather rudimentary. I wanted him to respect me and help me start on the project that obsessed me.

The National Security Agency, where I once worked, was a large building consisting of several storeys above ground and one below ground dedicated to incarcerating traitors. There was no sign or other indication that this was a security building, but everyone knew what it was. It was located halfway down a dirt road in an upscale neighbourhood of the capital. I was obliged to take a taxi there and had difficulty finding one. I paid the aged driver the amount he requested without trying to haggle; his chatter had given me a headache as he compared our dismal times to the awesome past. I went into the building to look for R.J., because I felt certain that he was one of the two men who had escorted the novelist from the Qasr al-Jummayz coffeehouse and who had been characterised as idiots, because I had glimpsed him hovering around the last time I was there. I had pretended not to see him, because I hadn't wanted to greet someone who was perhaps known to the people I wanted to meet. They might know what he did for a living. Then I would have been barred from their table before I could learn the strategies of writing – certainly not on account of his respectable profession, but because of the public perception of it.

R.J. was there and shook my hand warmly. He was surprised to see me back and no doubt assumed that I was in the service again.

'No, it's not what you think. I want to ask about the novelist A.T.'

He raised his eyebrows in astonishment. 'Is he a relative?'

'Not at all, but his situation concerns me.'

I didn't say how his situation concerned me, because I knew that these soldiers – and I had been one of them until recently – knew nothing about novels except that they are frequently a disgusting component in acts of treason against the nation. I wasn't a traitor; I was a writer at the beginning of his career.

My colleague informed me that the novelist's file, entitled 'The Slaughtered Bird', had left his hands and been referred to the official who would rule on his case. He wasn't accused or even suspected of anything; this was just an ordinary procedure we take from time to time to remind people that we exist and are keen to defend the nation's security and its welfare. The official knew me very well because I had been a member of his team for a number of years during which my service had been exemplary. As a matter of fact, he had been fond of me, and I knew that he had vigorously opposed my forced retirement and had intended to find me a position where I wouldn't need two legs to run or even to walk, but his opposition hadn't proved successful. The official was very busy, and many people were entering and leaving his office. I saw some old suspects I knew and some new ones I had never seen before led trembling to his office. Even so, he set aside his chores for a few minutes to listen to me. I asked him quite tersely to release the slaughtered bird from his cage for the sake of Abdullah Farfar and his exemplary service. He didn't ask why. He summoned one of the men posted in front of his desk and entrusted the mission to him. Then he rose to shake my hand. I left the agency's building with my head held high. Eva's taste was strong in my mouth then and so was my intention to begin writing. At the door I was obliged to bring out my big cotton handkerchief and cover half of my face with it because the novelist A.T. was there shaking the dirt from his shirt. As he headed out of the door, his shoulder brushed against mine.

That same evening we were circling round the novelist at the table that would witness the first opinion I had expressed about a book. I was near the writer. The woman with the faded jeans was radiant now, unlike that morning, and closer to him than I was: she was so close she was almost inside his ribcage. The young man who carried two books and other people I was seeing for the first time were congratulating him on his return after an absence of several days. He didn't answer any of the questions about where he had been. I was smiling to myself, knowing full well that a man we take and then return to society remains our prisoner, even when he is completely free. I knew that the novelist would direct the conversation to other topics and might deny he had a problem. Had witnesses not seen him arrested, no one would have known. I smiled slyly, feeling proud that I was the person who had liberated him and that he was mine at that moment, even if this was a special form of possession unknown to anyone but me.

He was saying, 'Friends, I have a new work in mind and have begun to delineate its features. I'll write a novel about a football player in a poor neighbourhood who suddenly finds himself a government minister. What do you think?'

'Everything you write is a big event, Master.'

That was the woman in faded jeans speaking. She was still near the writer's ribs. I could detect on her face telltale signs of a desire to ask him about her novel *A Moment of Love*, even though she knew full well that he hadn't been in a situation that allowed him to read.

'I read *Eva Died in My Bed*; it's a totally new experiment and awe-inspiring. I want to congratulate you on that.'

I, Abdullah Farfar, made that big statement – as if I

knew all the experimental novels and could sort out the brand-new works from old ones. *I've already admitted that* Eva *was the first novel I ever read and that I understood some of it but not the rest. But don't worry about that – I have a right to talk.* The writer was about to respond to my praise, raising his head, which had regained its arrogance, but I quickly asked him the question I had held in reserve since I finished *Eva*: 'But why did the hero suddenly leave Eva, that enchanting woman he had worn himself out chasing, and go to Sansha Marov, who had been chasing him even though he ignored her all the time?'

'This is left to the reader's discretion, Brother Nuruddin – he's the one who will judge the hero's conduct after reading the novel. Not I . . . I wrote it and that's that.'

'My name's Abdullah Harfash . . . Abdullah Farfar,' I quickly pointed out, sensing that he had deliberately forgotten my name and invented another one for me that didn't resemble mine or come close to it; the girl in jeans had done precisely the same thing when I met her that morning. He could have said 'Brother' without adding Nuruddin. I wished I could have informed him that he owed his freedom to my intervention, that I had made his arrogant round table possible, and that I had seen him when his shirt was caked with dirt and his nose was directed down at the ground. One of the guards had told me he had got down on his knees to beg for a cigarette. But I couldn't. That would ruin everything, including my novel which was about to be written.

'Another question, Master. Are all those real events? I mean – did they actually happen? And are those characters real people?'

'Naturally not everything that is written is real, Brother Farfar. There's reality and then there's the imagination. A successful work makes the reader think that the imaginary is real. You've made some attempts at writing . . . I believe you told us that.'

'Yes, I've made some attempts. I'll share them with you in the near future.' I spoke confidently, and incoherent ideas began to bounce around in my mind. All I had to do was broaden my imagination and be patient, then I would imitate the novelist A.T.'s writing rituals, which he had mentioned previously. I would imitate all of them to see which ritual granted me something; perhaps I would have my own rituals in the future. The gathering was breaking up; I shuffled away without anyone looking at my wooden leg. They had no doubt grown accustomed to its appearance and the way it dragged across the floor. In the near future they would become accustomed to my voice, which would debate with them more.

*Chapter Nine*

This wasn't a normal evening in my house when I took my first step on the path to writing, adopting the ritual of elegance after I retrieved my grey suit, which had been altered, from the tailor Kh.R. He delivered it to me after fifteen days – steam-cleaned and expertly ironed. I spread it out in front of him and examined it deliberately for fear it might have been soiled by grease that sprinkled from the sandwiches he ate while sewing. I couldn't think of any elegant hotel where I could sit in the lobby and write, nor was I travelling so I could write in the departure hall of an airport, which according to A.T. is an inspirational place. Instead, I decorated my living room with a number of additional vases and two pieces of crystal that I purchased from a shop called Tobia for Chandeliers and Crystal. The scent of a mint air freshener pervaded the room, making it inspirational. From the wall opposite a picture of me when I was fifteen kept watch. In it I was holding a bow I once used to hunt birds. Next to it was a picture of my late mother sitting on a rope bed and holding a palm leaf fan.

My day had been very full ever since I had set out early in the morning, stumbling and shuffling with my vile leg. I enquired about the leftist M.M., the used-car dealer, utilising my expert detective skills, and learned that he had studied the culinary arts in Moscow where he specialised in cooking slices of meat marinated in tomato sauce with basil. He hadn't pursued his specialisation as a career, however, and it had merely been a degree he hung in his house. Politics swept him up for a long period before he abandoned that for the car business. I discovered that I had known all this before, when I had shadowed him for a long time. Apparently, I had forgotten all these things either because of the passage of time or because of my craving to enter the world of writing. M.M. certainly wasn't the hero of *Eva*, and their stories weren't similar. He had married one of his relatives and lives in a working-class neighbourhood far removed from any violets and gardenias or the bed strewn with legends. The imagination is one thing, and reality is something else. That's what A.T. said, and perhaps he's right.

Unexpected guests visited me at noon, and I was bewildered by their visit. I invited them in and seated them in the living room. I offered them tabaldi fruit juice, which I always keep mixed and ready, because I like it a lot. My guests were Aunt Th. and her husband, the sports masseur, who had recovered completely from overdosing on Ativan. He was wearing his old sweat outfit and his sports shoes without any laces. He had pinned his tin medal to his sweatshirt along with another one he had commissioned from a metalworker who specialised in making trinkets. His name was inscribed on it and just below that: 'Hero of *"Perfumed Sealing Wax"*'. What really surprised me even more was that the cheerleader-gravedigger A.D. accompanied them. I learned that he had brought them to my house after going to complain about me to them.

Before I could say anything, al-Mudallik addressed me in his gruff voice and struck me on the shoulder with a hand like a stick of dry firewood. I felt more alarm than pain. 'Farfar, give the man back his newspaper. You can't appropriate the keepsakes of a living man. Give it back at once.'

'What newspaper?' I raised my eyebrows in disbelief.

'The one containing photos of the party honouring him. He accuses you of stealing it and attempting to alter it to replace his picture with yours. Return the man's pictures immediately, Farfar,' al-Mudallik repeated. At the same moment he pulled from his pocket one of those hand-cut pieces of paper that he had distributed to visitors who had come to reassure themselves about his health while he was ill. This time it was red. He held it before my face for a moment before placing it in my hand.

Then I was able to read the inscription: 'To Abdullah Farfar, my in-law who has never let me down. Thanks for your admiration.'

'This is brilliant, isn't it? I cut it out especially for you.'

The cheerleader-gravedigger was sitting shakily on the edge of his chair. He was dressed in his green Sufi robe with the string of hyacinth bean prayer beads dangling from his neck and the rheumatism bracelet around his right wrist. His eyes looked dazed – the eyes of a madman or a malaria patient with a high fever. Aunt Th. was also sitting silently on her chair.

I shouted passionately, 'What's this nonsense? Why would I need a madman's photos badly enough to steal them? Have you forgotten who I am?'

Suddenly I remembered that I actually had taken his paper the day when he had departed without noticing that he had left it on the ground beside that distant rock where he had been sitting. I truly hadn't stolen it but had held onto it for his sake, feeling certain that he would return to ask for it one day. It had never occurred to me that he would ask for it in this weird way. The cheerleader-gravedigger had no doubt lost his mind. If only they had never honoured him . . . If only! He would have continued to be a great cheerleader and a gravedigger at the Umran Cemetery to the end of his days. I rose and headed to my inner room where I had stored the paper, which was covered in a thick layer of dust. I shook it and handed it to the cheerleader silently. He took it, stood up, and departed. He walked away as if he were lost in a desert, turning right and then left. In a calm voice I tried to explain to al-Mudallik what had happened, but he silenced me with his gruff voice: 'Even if he is insane, as you claim, he has personal mementoes and recognises them easily. Come on, woman. Let's go.'

He grasped my aunt's hand roughly as he rose. His face was gleaming and freshly shaven, and he was smoking a local Bringi brand cigarette. My aunt wasn't her usual self and allowed herself to be led about docilely. She had said nothing from the time she arrived until she left. Perhaps she had been blown away by the primal way he had fainted on stage, even though she hadn't witnessed it, or perhaps she feared losing him now that women had started to take an interest in him. I had noticed that his fellow thespian who had played the part of his lost love sat very close to his bed during his convalescence in the hospital. She was a young woman who had been made up to look like an old woman meeting an aged lover. *I don't know. I don't know exactly.*

The certainty that I would write about al-Mudallik increased. If he wasn't a character in this novel that obsessed me, I would definitely put him in another novel I would produce later. He was an incredibly rich character, as I had heard them describe this type of character in the Qasr al-Jummayz. The gravedigger could also become a character – a sensible, widely known person who loses his mind after being honoured by the president of the country – my God! A broad imagination could turn him into a treasure all by himself.

I had experienced many things during my service, as I have mentioned. Some of these made me happy because I had done my duty for my country; others might have saddened me because I had wronged someone or robbed a man of his future. In our work, however, there is no room for sorrow, and we are trained to cancel out sadness. I know a colleague who led his paternal uncle to a square where he was executed, knowing full well that the soldiers weren't using paper bullets. The penitent prostitute in Saigon had, no doubt, been a sinner. I had engaged in experiments, not sins. I began to search my mind for some of those experiences that might fit the ritual of elegance, the ritual of wearing my altered grey suit and grasping the black Parker pen filled with ink, while seated with a notebook of yellow paper in front of me waiting for me to write something on it. *Al-Mudallik and the gravedigger – I'll try writing about them with the nude ritual or the ritual of wandering the streets. I won't wade into the muck of the zar singer Ammuna al-Bayda', because there is no way at present that I could rent her house and her trance sessions.* Stealing a wallet from a livestock dealer or a handbag from a woman walking down the street and writing from inside prison – I dismissed all this from my mind entirely. My past wouldn't allow me to embark on an experiment like this, not even if I did it without stealing and relied on acquaintances who are prison guards.

Then an idea came – it came suddenly, by God – and I rose to dance giddily, forgetting that my wooden leg wasn't strapped on and was instead resting on the chair opposite me. I had removed it precisely to force myself to focus on my work and not move about. I almost fell but wasn't upset. I'll write about the case of the secretary Sh.N.

This was known in our agencies as the case of 'The Apple', because the heroine kept chewing on apples even while undergoing harsh interrogation. I had witnessed the real facts of this case more than ten years earlier. *I'll change the names, the way novelists do, and try to be imaginative. I'll try.* I seized the Parker pen and leaned over my papers. As I wrote, the night passed, and hundreds of demons wrote with me.

*Chapter Ten*

'I kept her under close surveillance that morning. I was standing at the corner of the street opposite the building where she worked as a secretary for the Delta Noon Livestock Export Company. I wore a tunic with sleeves I had torn myself. I had donned a pair of Persol sunglasses after smashing one of the lenses to make them look old. A beggar carrying a palm leaf basket on his back passed and asked for alms, but I didn't give him anything. He entered the building. A woman wearing a lot of gold around her neck and arms passed me and said, "As-salam alaykum", and entered. A man got out of an old taxi with a broken door. The driver didn't look like a real cabby because he wore green velvet pants and was playing a tape of one of the new singers. I heard the song "Bahdala . . . affront", which had become popular recently, coming from his taxi. The man entered the building, and the sham cabby drove off. Two hours later the secretary Sh.N. left the building, holding an apple with about three bites taken from it. She was accompanied by the beggar, the woman wearing all the gold, and the man who had climbed out of the taxi. They were laughing, but suddenly Sh.N. turned towards me at a time when the street was becoming more congested, because many firms are located in that area. She stopped laughing, and I clearly heard her tell her comrades that there would be "no sugar in the coffee today". I didn't understand her phrase and guessed it was a predetermined code. I watched them separate, each going his own way. Then the secretary went back into the building again. I stood there until noon brooding about her cryptic phrase and waiting for her to emerge, but she didn't. I came back the next morning, this time wearing dapper clothing – a blue shirt with black trousers and a red necktie. I carried the day's edition of the newspaper *The Parrot*, which specialises in criticism of the government and is printed and distributed clandestinely, although we know how. The beggar appeared again and requested alms, which I gave him this time. The woman with all the gold arrived, dressed in a gauzy violet thaub with a white stripe at the hem to show it was an expensive number from Rad. The man disembarked from the same taxi with the broken door, and the tape of the song "Bahdala . . . affront" was still playing. The man entered the building, and the driver moved off. I vacillated for some time between entering the building or continuing my stake-out. I wasn't able to pull my walkie-talkie from inside my clothing to consult the agency for fear of attracting attention . . . and . . .'

'Just a minute . . . please stop, Harfash-Farfar.'

The novelist A.T. was addressing me in a quavering voice, and I noticed then the frightened look in his eyes.

His knees were trembling too, and beads of sweat glistened on his face while he twisted around as if searching for something he had lost.

I had hunted him down methodically that day, waiting for him at the door of the Qasr al-Jummayz since early in the morning, before any of his admirers arrived, especially that girl in jeans – I sensed that she didn't appreciate my presence among them and that by sitting next to the writer's ribs she might spoil my plan to learn how to write. I wanted him to listen to my opening, which I had laboured over all through the previous night, clad in my suit that had been altered to fit me by the tailor Kh.R. and recording it in my pitiful handwriting on my yellow paper, which was previously reserved for reports. *Employing the ritual of elegance, I'll write a novel called* The Apple. *It's the tale of the beautiful secretary who worked as an operative for a network of traitors dedicated to the destruction of public security. We were able to frustrate their plan at an appropriate time.* The novelist arrived pompously with a cigarette in his mouth and found me in front of him. I wanted to see him alone, to keep our meeting secret, and to gain his admiration or advice so I could produce an excellent novel. I would return later to read it to the others in the Qasr al-Jummayz. I entreated him to accompany me to another location so I could show him my opening section. After quite a sales pitch on my part, he agreed while looking at a large gold wristwatch shaped like a heart.

We sat down at an extremely dirty table in a coffeehouse

called al-Bi'r or 'The Well'. It was definitely one of worst coffeehouses in the capital. It was a filthy watering hole, and most of its patrons were desert men – camel traders who came to the capital from time to time to conduct business, visit the hospitals, or put their fortunes in the banks. They relaxed in coffeehouses like this and carried on conversations with rancorous voices and lewd words. At precisely that moment one of them was discussing camel breeding in a loud voice accompanied by libertine laughter. He was describing how the male camel mounts the female and what happens next. I wasn't the one who had chosen this coffeehouse, and the novelist hadn't either. When walking had exhausted my vile leg and I could feel it wobbling, we had been at the doors of The Well.

'Who are you?'

His voice rocked me severely; I don't know why. These were clearly words that he was not using to ask me to complete my novel. He was no doubt jealous of me, sensing that I was a writer who might shake his renown if I persevered; so he wished to silence me. I didn't want to make any further conjectures but wished to know his thinking.

'I'm Abdullah Harfash . . . Abdullah Farfar. You know that.'

'I mean: what's your identity?'

'I don't understand, Master.'

His knees had stopped trembling but alarm was still apparent in his eyes, and there were more beads of sweat on his face. I noticed that he was summoning the waiter, who was busy laughing savagely with the camel traders, to order a coffee without sugar, even though a cup of coffee without sugar stood untouched before him.

'What you just read me isn't the beginning of a novel; it's a police report.'

He had unmasked me, no doubt . . . uncovered me . . . found me out. Unconsciously I had channelled a numb-skull, not the novelist, while writing. This was the same report that I had written about the actual stake-out more than ten years ago and that could still be found in the file labelled 'The Apple' in the agency. It had leapt onto the yellow pages without me being aware of that. Only now I remembered; I wished desperately that I could find some way out of this predicament. How . . . how . . .? I was close to tears at that moment. I didn't want the idea of writing the novel to desert me after I had put so much groundwork into the project. I wasn't in the service, but the cursed parasite of the secret service might still emerge at any time. Certainly the only way out of this mess was to reveal everything to the novelist candidly. Perhaps he would continue to encourage me.

He asked again, 'What have I done to deserve the honour of your surveillance, sir? I enjoyed four days of your hospitality during which all my ideas fled. Now, an author of police reports – a man with a wooden leg – reads *Eva Died in My Bed* and sits at my table holding a discussion with me. Your modus operandi has evolved . . .

It has really advanced. Everyone will be surprised when they learn this – especially our friend, the creative woman.'

He mentioned the name S., and I surmised that this was the impetuous girl with the faded jeans. I was surprised to hear him refer to her as 'the creative woman', given that he had received the manuscript of her novel that day with obvious disdain. He rose to leave, evincing no desire to hear my reply. I grabbed hold of his clothing so hard that the camel traders thought we were having a quarrel and raised their sticks to break it up. I begged him to sit back down so I could explain. When he finally agreed and did take a seat, he ordered coffee without sugar for a third time, even though he hadn't touched the two cups in front of him.

I recounted everything to him: my former employment in the National Security Agency; my freak accident when we were on a stake-out on a road leading to a suspicious farm, the loss of my leg; the death of one of my colleagues and the palsy that the third member of our team had contracted with no cure in sight; the Bengali flower vendor who was in Nice when he wrote a novel; the man who was a poor cobbler in Rwanda when he wrote; the penitent prostitute in Saigon and her terrific income; the persistence of this mad idea that I should write a novel; and finally what I had done about it. I didn't include any details about al-Mudallik, Aunt Th.'s husband, the cheerleading gravedigger, or any of the other personalities I had encountered during my life and believed fit characters for fiction, because I feared they might be stolen. Anyone possessing the sharpened tools that A.T., for example, had used to write *Eva* and other novels, could steal my characters and write them up in a way that I wouldn't be able to pick them out of his texts. He certainly listened to me, and I was about to tell him that I had sprung him from the hospitality he had mentioned but then sensed that he had totally relaxed; he drank the three cups of coffee in one draught each and didn't order another.

'Fine, Farfar-Harfash. I truly believe you. In fact, I congratulate you on this big change.'

Smiling, he placed his hand affectionately on my shoulder. I sensed at that moment that he was a genuine writer who would overlook any potentially embarrassing information I told him and that he respected my new desire for change. He would definitely encourage me to develop my imagination and my command of language. I loved him now and hoped we would become friends. At that time I relaxed totally. We actually were friends, friends having a pleasant chat.

'Do you know an insect's stages of development, Farfar?'

'I've forgotten them. They were in a science lesson in elementary school.'

'I'll remind you. The egg develops into a larva, which is a minute creature that then turns into a pupa inside a cocoon. Next the creature emerges as an imago – a mature insect. Remember now?'

'Yes . . . yes.'

'The larva – or grub – may grow or die before developing

further. The insect really cannot protect its larvae from dying young, but you can.'

'I don't understand, Master.'

I really didn't grasp what he meant and couldn't find any link between writing novels and the stages of development of insects. *I'll listen until I get it.*

'I'm comparing writing to the developmental stages of insects. You wrote a grub that will never grow into a pupa and complete its cycle. This secret police report is just a dead grub that emerged from your mind stillborn. Try to develop it through the remainder of its stages. Do you understand now?'

I actually didn't understand it very well. I did grasp that writing required a lot more culture than I possessed at the time. Reading about magicians' feats or people's marriage practices wasn't an adequate cultural background. Reading one novel I had only partially understood wasn't a whole lot of culture. I would need to strive to attain greater cultural literacy before writing a novel. I wasn't at all upset to have my first attempt compared to a stillborn grub. It didn't bother me that my future attempts would also be larvae. I could try to alter that vile security report that had exposed me and transform it into a genuine beginning filled with imagination. I might also tear it up and try other rituals that might bring me a beginning in which al-Mudallik, Aunt Th.'s husband, and the cheerleader-gravedigger A.D. might figure. The good news was that I hadn't allowed this meeting to make me miserable or dejected, even when I was described as the author of police reports and a man with a wooden leg. Perhaps this despicable leg was a distinction that set me apart from other people instead of being a curse. I realised that it might help when I was roaming the streets to research a homeless novel. In that lengthy meeting between me and the novelist A.T., who no longer seemed to be in any hurry and refrained from consulting his watch, I learned many things about him that I hadn't known. He was quite a simple person who hid behind a facade of arrogance; he had worked as a maths teacher in middle schools and left teaching when he caught the writing bug. He had read a lot, he told me, before he wrote, and had travelled a lot. He possessed a huge library that he would show me one day. He actually resembled me in one respect: he had never married.

'Soon you won't need to borrow my rituals to write. You'll gradually discover your own.'

*By God . . . very encouraging talk, but all the same I'll try his other rituals – the naked and homeless rituals – and show him the grubs I produce.* He appeared more than willing to sit with me and listen to me at any time, in this very same coffeehouse, al-Bi'r, far from 'the choir' – as he called his other companions who attended his sessions at the Qasr al-Jummayz.

He said, 'This is the first time I've been here, and I like it. No pesky reader will stumble across you here; moreover it contains many points of inspiration. Look.'

I turned towards the desert camel traders. One of them

had removed his goatskin sandals, put them on the floor, and climbed onto a table. He knelt on it, lifted his tunic, revealing dirty pants, and began screeching. He was imitating a she-camel in labour. His mates were laughing, and the coffeehouse's only waiter was standing motionless to observe this ritual. I laughed and the novelist did too.

'What about the novel *A Moment of Love* by your friend whom you termed a creative woman? She gave you a copy of the manuscript; is it a dead grub or a fully developed insect?' I asked this, feeling ecstatic that I had gained the friendship of a luminary author, who just an hour earlier had been about to destroy me.

'Listen, Farfar: the topic of larvae and things like that applies to you and not to beautiful girls with wide eyes. A girl's larva is equivalent to your adult insect. This is what we call the benefit of beauty.'

'So, you will write a preface for her? Isn't that right?'

'I don't know. I'll find some way to escape from writing that preface; otherwise I'll write circumspectly.'

I told him about the leftist M.M. who became a used-car dealer and how I had wondered at first whether he was the hero of the superb novel *Eva*. I added some imaginative touches to his story and took care to make him seem quite different from the hero. A.T. laughed, and his teeth reminded me of those of al-Mudallik, Aunt Th.'s husband; they were the teeth of a long-time smoker, perhaps one who had started smoking early in life, before he learned how to write. His tenth cigarette – a local Bringi brand one – was burning between his fingers. He hadn't known M.M. and had only visited Moscow for the first time two years ago when one of his novels was translated into Russian. Inspired by the sights that had dazzled him there, he had returned from that trip to write *Eva Died in My Bed*. When he asked me whether I had known him for a long time and shadowed him, I strongly denied it. I actually hadn't specialised in the surveillance of novelists in particular or of cultural figures in general. My first real sighting of A.T. had been the day I came to Qasr al-Jummayz in search of him. I had heard about him but not much and not often. The information he gave about himself may well be recorded in our agency, but I hadn't known any of it.

The proprietor of the coffeehouse had noticed the presence of strangers in the midst of the chaos of his desert and rustic patrons with whom he was familiar – people who no longer excited his interest. We saw him leave his seat behind the till uncomfortably and approach us. From my long experience observing human discomfort I felt certain that he was apprehensive about something and wanted to reassure himself; perhaps he was engaging in an activity that warranted concern. He said, 'Welcome, welcome', and drew a chair to our table and sat down. His smile revealed gold teeth carefully strung across his mouth. He sounded like a nervous maiden, and a very large ring set with a green turquoise gleamed on his left hand. Rising and prompting me to rise, the novelist said, 'Consider him carefully, Farfar. He might qualify as one of your grubs.'

## Chapter Eleven

I didn't visit the A'laf Bookstore to buy any particular book this time. I was filled with a desire to possess a bookcase with a number of shelves packed with books – like the one I had seen in the home of the novelist A.T., who took me there yesterday to show me how he reads and writes. We met once more in al-Bi'r Coffeehouse, where we saw a new group of desert men practise the same rituals we had previously observed, and a group of rustic northerners with a different set of rituals. One of them was playing the tambour, which is widely distributed across the north. The proprietor of the coffeehouse spoke to us, and we conversed with him. He actually is a suitable character for a novel. A.T. confirmed this when he recalled one of the characters of his novel *The Residents of the Sa'd District Under Occupation*, which he said he had written in prison, while contemplating the man's clean-shaven face, his eyes, which were expertly outlined with kohl, and his golden smile, which never left his face during the minutes he sat with us. After the man left us to return to his normal seat, A.T. suggested, 'You could make him either the victim or the victimiser. He would work well as either.'

'How?'

'The victim is a person who falls into a carefully laid trap without knowing it, and repeatedly falls into more traps until he becomes accustomed to falling. The victimiser is a person who deliberately walks into the trap and continues looking for traps all his life. What do you think?'

'What's your opinion, Master?'

'I see him as a victim. If I used him as a character, I would give him a disturbed childhood in a broken home as part of a family with a harsh and quarrelsome father and an irresponsible mother who leaves her children and flees to a brothel. I would have him live in a neighbourhood filled with wounds – hundreds of booby traps that could have affected his condition.'

This was really challenging talk for my mind; the craft of writing became increasingly complicated every day. What the novelist had said flowed easily from his tongue but would have been extremely difficult for me to express. I know a lot of people like the owner of the coffeehouse, men perhaps even more languid and disturbed than he is, people I knew when I was a young child, classmates in school, and neighbours in the district where I grew up, but no one referred to them as victims or victimisers, and we never attempted to search for the environment that had shaped them into this or that. Something from reality . . . something from the imagination – and you create your book. The proprietor of the coffeehouse sitting across the room from us was a vivid reality, but it would take the kind of imagination that assumed a mature mind to write him up in a way that was true to him.

I entered the A'laf Bookstore carrying a wallet crammed with pounds I had counted out meticulously. I was dreaming of buying at least ten books at once as the first nucleus of my nascent library. I was stunned when I saw the novelist's library; I definitely couldn't imagine that anyone could have read all those books. Some were about sciences that were unrelated to novels, like medicine, geography, and even astronomy. But why would he purchase them if he wasn't ever going to read them? He had certainly read them. He had become a respected writer thanks to this reading.

'You again, Abdullah Farfar? Did you find something to indict the author for in the novel *Eva?*' The Christian R.M. was addressing me with the same new-found impertinence that he had learned following my forced retirement – forgetting our putative friendship that had lasted for many years. He didn't seem convinced that I was a reader and a new customer for his bookstore or that I came in search of nothing more than the enjoyment of reading. A few people of quite different ages were browsing the shelves of books, leafing through some books carefully and casting a quick glance at others. I noticed the middle-aged man who had bought the book *Sex in Our Lives*. He was clutching another book called *Your Sex Life After Fifty* and seemed eager to pay for it. A new video was playing on the old TV placed in a corner of the bookstore. The owner of the bookstore appeared in it attired in a green suit and wearing an imported tie. He was speaking in an opinion survey conducted by a local television station of a number of book exhibitors, and discussing a book that described the redoubtable culture of ancient China that had recently arrived in his bookstore.

'I told you: I'm out of the service. You know that.'

'Yes . . . out of the service, I know.'

He said that indifferently and left to inspect the middle-aged man's wallet, which had just opened. I noticed that there was hardly any money in it and that the man took all of it out to pay for the book. I tried to feel sorry for the man but couldn't. It will take me a long time to habituate myself to feeling emotions. I headed directly to the rack of novels and began to gaze at them as if they were cute girls swimming in a pond. I started to cull through the titles; some I liked and others I didn't. When I finished my selection, I handed the Christian the amount he requested and left, ignoring the look of surprise in his eyes. *Tomorrow he'll learn everything when my printed book arrives for him to display in his bookstore.* I carried away a full bag of fodder. I considered the Christian owner of the bookstore from the viewpoint of the novelist A.T. He was neither a victim nor a victimiser, but a stolid man who traded in books, both legal and illegal ones, naked and cloaked ones. If he was destined to become a character in a book, he would be written up in the style of a police report as a dead grub: a stolid but shifty and impetuous man ready to die for his beliefs. That's perhaps how he seems to me with my fumbling imagination, but for the novelist A.T., the bookstore owner would have a strange past and a stranger future. I decided to ask the novelist and see what he said. At that moment I recalled that I had recorded that same description of a bookseller in a very old report still on file in his folder in our agency.

In one of the woodworking shops near where I was living, I managed to find a small wooden bookcase composed of five shelves, and the carpenter sold it to me for a reasonable price. I transported it home on the roof of a motorised rickshaw after tying it down firmly with ropes. The rickshaw driver seemed grumpy and was worried about it shaking around on the roof. He stopped every so often to reassure himself that it was still securely fastened before continuing on his way.

I was in the living room of my house gazing at my nascent library after arranging the books, which barely filled half of the first shelf of the bookcase. My library would grow in size; it would definitely get bigger and fill the rest of the shelves. I would reserve one shelf for the novels I would write. I was smiling, because I saw that my imagination was running wild. The novel that obsessed me had become several novels, perhaps because I had moved so close to the world of writing. I borrowed the luminary novelist from his choir of admirers frequently and sat alone with him in al-Bi'r Coffeehouse, surrounded by all its strange inspirations including the effeminate proprietor, who might be a victim or a victimiser. The girl S. who wore jeans had already told the novelist once in Qasr al-Jummayz, without paying any heed to me, that she found it odd for him to befriend someone no one knew anything about, even now, or understood how he had suddenly appeared in their world. The novelist didn't reply. In my imagination I slapped her – yes, I slapped her and wished I could tell her about larvae theory and that her novel *A Moment of Love* was actually a stillborn grub that would never have become a fully developed insect had it not been for her black eyes. The novelist A.T. referred to this as the advantage of beauty. I scrutinised the girl's face carefully and didn't discover enough beauty to justify her leap over the stages of bug development. Many traces of pimples were still visible despite the thick layers of powder and cleansing creams with which her face was anointed.

*Chapter Twelve*

I stood in front of Aunt Th.'s house and gazed at the satellite dishes that totally covered the flat roof terrace and that rested against large rusty poles. I was brooding about the fuss made about them and the harm they could cause the people who rent their roofs for these installations. Al-Mudallik had told me once that they were a boon a person couldn't easily acquire. I don't know if that's really true, and the row about them hadn't been settled yet.

I told the novelist A.T. about al-Mudallik, my aunt's husband, and the great inspiration he could be. I also told him about the cheerleader-cum-gravedigger A.D. and the insanity to which he succumbed after he had been honoured at the behest of the country's president. I told him after I learned to trust him and felt sure he wouldn't steal from me any character I wanted to write about. Quite the contrary – he offered me characters and encouraged me to continue trying to write about the proprietor of al-Bi'r Coffeehouse whenever we sat alone there. At Qasr al-Jummayz, as well, we had a similar whispered conversation after we had finished listening to three whole chapters of the author S.'s novel, *A Moment of Love*, which was to be released soon by a local publishing house with A.T.'s extremely cautious preface that gave beauty its due, even though I had never felt that her beauty merited any reward. The girl read in a voice unlike her normal speech. She added many pauses, breaks, and weepy echoes and kept moving her right hand, which didn't hold the manuscript, placing it on her heart, her belly, and her wavy hair, which – once her multicoloured scarf slipped – I noticed had been tinted dark brown. She was a rash girl, and her novel was a grub. The group gasped with admiration after each sentence, and I was forced to gasp too, copying everyone else. No one was drinking tea or coffee or smoking, and none of the Ethiopian waitresses was hovering around the area. The table where we sat had been cordoned off with a metal barrier, which was painted white, to prevent curious onlookers from disturbing the reading; this had been done at the girl's request. I heard some expressions that I couldn't understand or digest. In a story with an engaging plot I would never expect to hear phrases like: 'Adorn me with jewels if I'm a sultana or bind me with ropes and lash me with whips if I'm a slave, sultan of sultans . . .' or like this: 'within your eyes, desire lies dormant; rouse it from its torpor. Awaken it, I entreat you . . . I want it awake and stupid; I love stupidity.' I almost burst out laughing when the girl bent her whole body over to touch the floor. Then, weeping, she raised her head a little from the manuscript and declared, 'This was the cruellest bout of weeping in my life, a moment when the grenade of sorrow exploded inside my rosy happiness . . . observe the severed fragments of happiness . . . see how they lie scattered here and there . . . and there's no paramedic or physician.' I could have laughed, but the remainder of the choir moaned and their hands applauded loudly.

The novelist leaned towards me to whisper while the girl S. was busy receiving felicitations from her friends, who could finally breathe – like the novelist A.T. himself. I had told him about al-Mudallik and the gravedigger and other personalities I had met in my life. He said, 'Pay attention to al-Mudallik. Befriend him. Make a serious effort to become acquainted with his past and with his aspirations. You may come up with something.'

Aunt Th. opened the door. She seemed to be looking younger and was wearing the blouse of a girl of twenty. It had stripes and colours and a V-neck. Meanwhile her hair had been expertly dyed black. She preceded me into her house. Her sandals had high heels; I had never seen her wear anything like that before. *I won't brood about my aunt's new behaviour; she must have adopted it to please a demented husband who almost died in a role not worth dying for.* Al-Mudallik was in the living room, lost in a white cloud of tobacco smoke, wearing his cotton Jil brand leisurewear. He was playing around with the TV's remote control, flipping channels without pausing on any of them. I saw palm readers, vocalists, a bicycle race, an American hug, and other things appear and disappear in quick succession. The iron medal that was embossed with the words '*Perfumed Sealing Wax*' dangled down his chest.

When he noticed me standing in front of him, he yelled, 'Congratulate me, Abdullah – I've landed a new part in a play, called *The Death of a Dolt*, which is going to be performed soon at the Civic Youth Theatre.'

I felt intensely alarmed, not for his sake, naturally, but for my own. I was afraid I would become entangled in another of his seizures or an actual death this time and not be able to read or write. He himself was now the axis of the new novel I shall begin. I'm going to write a lot so I can surprise A.T. with it. I want to learn things I don't know from him. Then I'll kindle my imagination and see what kind of grub emerges.

'Don't tell me you're the dolt who dies in the play!'

'I wish I were, Farfar. If only I were! I would die a thousand times better than that failure who calls himself an actor.'

I felt relieved. In fact I sighed deeply as I sat down beside him. 'But what's your part in the play?'

'It is actually a big part even though some superficial people might think it's an insignificant role. I'm one of two men who carry away the litter containing the dolt after he dies. Isn't this an excellent part with a lot of action?'

I actually didn't know what to reply; al-Mudallik's question lingered between the two of us waiting for an answer. His eyes were staring me straight in the face, and his hand, which was like a dry stick of firewood, was rapping me on the shoulder, causing me more alarm than pain. I couldn't laugh, even though the situation was ludicrous. Any birdbrain janitor from the theatre staff would be able to carry a litter. Any tramp passing in the street during the performance could carry the litter. Any member of the audience who was asked to 'lend us a hand, brother' could extend his hand and carry the litter. I recalled once seeing two elephants in the zoo, which used to be in the centre of the capital, but which was closed to allow for development of its land, use their trunks to carry their keeper on a litter in a demonstration that everyone applauded. I don't know why, but I suddenly felt afraid that in that role al-Mudallik was hiding some surprise that would cause us all headaches.

'You haven't said what you think, Farfar. I suppose you don't like the part.'

*My mind was far from him, thinking about the treasure I possess but haven't been able to exploit yet.* If I drill on writing a little, I'll produce pearls from him. If only I were A. T. or if only he possessed my treasure, I would read a significant work.

'Wait until I see the part on stage; then I'll give you my opinion.'

Al-Mudallik appeared delighted, touched his iron medallion, and tossed the rest of his lit cigarette into the ashtray without extinguishing it. He summoned my aunt, who entered, bearing herself erect, and brought me a glass of tabaldi juice, which they know I like. She placed it before me.

'Tell Farfar about the other surprise. You tell him.'

My aunt sat down on the seat opposite us. She was blushing and looked even younger than when she had opened the door. She announced, 'We're going to spend two days in Dubai. Your uncle has acquired two free plane tickets and two nights in an excellent hotel. We're leaving tomorrow.'

This really was a surprise and a greater one than his carrying the litter. I had never conceived of my aunt or her husband, al-Mudallik, outside of their life, which they had never altered since they met and married, and which consisted of routine, temporary quarrels, and deep affection. Al-Mudallik loves my aunt, and she loves him. I'm a grub hunter charged with finding a grub that will grow into an insect. Al-Mudallik lifted the cotton cushion he had been leaning on and pulled out a yellow envelope with many stamps. Opening it, he waved two tickets from Etihad Airways in my face along with another piece of paper that must have been the voucher for their stay in the hotel. 'Congratulations, Uncle. Congratulations, Aunt.' I rose to shake their hands without feeling any curiosity about the source of financing for this unique trip. Al-Mudallik would tell me if he felt like it. *I'll put off questioning him – I mean questioning him about his childhood and youth and whatever other aspects of his life might provide inspiration for me – until he returns. I won't inscribe anything on my yellow papers until I feel totally confident I'm not writing a police report.* I had frequently been tempted by the idea of changing that paper. I actually obtained some white paper but shunned it once I felt it. The white paper didn't have any glow that would engage me.

When I approached my house, I suddenly remembered that I hadn't seen the cheerleader-gravedigger A.D. for some time, not since the day he had lodged a complaint against me, arriving with my aunt and her husband. He had sat on the edge of his chair trembling. Then he had taken his newspaper numbly and departed like a man lost in the desert, turning right and then left.

It was afternoon, and a match was scheduled for the stadium between rival teams, one of them the Lablab team for which A.D. was the chief cheerleader. I saw scattered around the area a number of vendors of lupin seeds, chickpeas, and sugar cane. A mob was trying to enter the stadium, and people were pushing each other aside with their hands and shoulders. There was apparently some problem about the tickets. I changed direction and headed to the stadium. I plunged into the crowd, shoving and being shoved, and eventually neared the ticket window. The ticket agent knew me very well, because I was a long-time neighbour of the stadium and frequently visited it with my yellow paper when pursuing a threat to public security. He must not have heard about my accident or retirement and didn't notice my despicable wooden leg, because as soon as he saw me there, he shouted, 'Make way for his honour Abdullah Harfash. Make way, gang.'

His use of the word 'honour', which he yelled out, had

a magic effect in a town that loves this word or, more accurately, fears it and trembles on hearing it. I found the passageway leading to the entry gate free even of dirt, discarded lupin seed bags, and cigarette packs. I didn't thank the ticket agent and doubt that he expected it. Not thanking people is the result of years of training – you don't ever thank anyone. You allow him to serve you and to thank you for that opportunity. I heard the agent call after me, 'Thanks, your honour. Many thanks for the honour.' At that time I felt cheated that I was no longer in the distinguished service (and was instead pursuing novelists and members of the intelligentsia, who until recently had merely been meagre files among all those with which our agency teemed and humiliated guests who knelt on all fours pleading when escorted to our dark corridors) and that my writing was still at the level of grubs that might never develop into real insects. *It won't be long before the ticket agent and the mob, which was carried away by his phrase 'your honour' and which swept clear the entry passage, learn I'm a nobody who has been drummed out of the service. After that I'll be treated the way the Christian KM., proprietor of the bookstore, and the tailor Kh.R treat me. I'll be Farfar, the man with the wooden leg.*

The match and the chaotic uproar got off to a rousing start. I headed straight to the area where the cheerleader A.D. usually sat – a corner in the people's stand. A sturdy rattan chair had been placed there and secured by an iron chain to an iron hook that he had embedded in the concrete riser. Everyone knew the spot, and no one else would sit there, no matter how crowded the stadium was, even if the cheerleader didn't come. I know that he has similar seats in all the stadiums of the capital. His seat was vacant, and there was no trace of the cheerleader.

I looked around, searching for him in that vast crowd, thinking that he had perhaps changed his seat or that he was walking around to relieve his tension. But there was no trace of him. In the past, the cheerleader had not attracted my attention; when I had seen him I had not even greeted him, leaving him the mission of greeting me. The situation was different now, and the cheerleader had become a mainstay of my writing. Since I plan to write about him, I must investigate his life the way I'm investigating that of al-Mudallik, my aunt's husband. One part reality and one part imagination – then the writing is excellent. In leafing through books I recently purchased from A'laf as a preliminary to reading them in their entirety – these books that constitute the nucleus of my library – I sensed the existence of reality and imagination striding cheek by jowl. That's how writing is done – any writing, not just A.T.'s writing.

Apparently I was blocking the view of a number of ardent fans who sat near A.D.'s vacant seat. They shouted at me to move away. In a tone that I adopted to mollify them, I said, 'I'm looking for the chief, please.'

'Chief' was the nickname by which A.D. was known by both the football world and the world of grieving mourners when they buried a deceased person whose grave he had dug.

'The chief?' someone shouted.

'The chief's in al-Qasr al-Abyad. Look for him there. Now please go away. You . . . You scumbag, you just made me miss the goal. You shoeshine boy, you lowlife.'

*Al-Qasr al-Abyad is the largest mental hospital in the capital and a real black hole.* I have temporarily lost the cheerleader-gravedigger. I won't grieve and will consider how to write about him.

*Chapter Thirteen*

'Al-Mudallik was raised in a deprived environment in the town of Sinka in the east of the country. His father was an itinerant vegetable vendor who used his raucous voice to advertise his produce. His mother contributed to the family budget by making yoghurt to sell to her neighbours. Al-Mudallik didn't love his father, whom he considered a tyrant. He had also frequently seen him seize a woman's hands while making a sale or touch her breasts. Al-Mudallik would tell his mother, who would get angry. Then his father would come and beat him. He had loved football since his youth and would escape from his house to play with children in the neighbourhood. He formed a team with his friends and called it "The Watercress". They played against teams from other neighbourhoods and made coloured paper trophies they presented to the winning team.'

I continued to read to the novelist A.T. in al-Bi'r Coffeehouse my account of al-Mudallik's life as he had narrated it to me when I visited him after he returned bedazzled with Aunt Th. from two extraordinary days of novel enjoyment in Dubai. He was wearing a new athletic jersey that read 'Etihad Airways' in squiggly letters, with the firm's logo next to its name. On his chest were three new iron medals that had been artistically shaped into red hearts. Inscribed on these was *Perfumed Sealing Wax*. A fourth medal dangled from his hand. Although I couldn't see the inscription, I guessed it read *The Death of a Dolt*, in honour of this drama – in which he plays the litter carrier for the deceased dolt – that would soon be performed at the Civic Youth Theatre. My aunt was splendidly attired. She wore the Etihad Airways logo as well, but on a generously proportioned blouse and skirt. The kohl that lined her eyes had been liberally applied. I drank some clear, Lipton brand tea with them; this was the first time I had seen it in their house. I accepted from my aunt the present they had brought me: a yellow, short-sleeve shirt with gleaming buttons. Embroidered in blue on it was the phrase: 'Ghulum Ikhlasi Hotel . . . you're home!'

Al-Mudallik spoke non-stop, talking about the clean, wide streets and elegant parks with trees he had never seen before; the eye-catching, fast, modern cars; and the Shaykh Zayed Road towers that blew his mind. He thought that the jinn must have built them – not human beings. He began to discuss the markets that were filled with everything, including prosthetic limbs totally unlike my wooden leg. He paused and then asked my aunt, 'Please tell him about the markets; women understand squandering money better than men.'

My aunt didn't say much and spent most of the time smiling, laughing, or pinching herself to make sure she wasn't dreaming. The fragrance of a heady perfume wafted from her person, and a polygonal glass bottle rested near her hand. I listened patiently to al-Mudallik. After more than an hour I was able to broach my topic, which I considered extremely urgent. I explained to him first what a novel is, saying that it's a laboriously written long story and doesn't succeed unless it blends reality and imagination. He snapped, 'Of course I know what a novel is. I read adventure novels when I was young and enjoyed *Arsène Lupin* and *Monte Cristo*. Have you forgotten that I'm an actor who reads plays before acting in them? Shame on you, Abdullah. Shame, Farfar.'

I actually had forgotten that he was an actor who had since early in his youth been chasing after dramatists and theatrical directors to urge them to give him any part; he must understand what a novel is – perhaps better than I had before I recently became cultured. I offered him my apology, which he accepted. Meanwhile his hand reached out from time to time to start the medals on his chest swaying or to slap my shoulder, causing me to feel alarmed. I told him that I was in the process of writing a novel and that he would no doubt play a part in it. Then he would become even more famous, and parts in plays would cascade down on him. Contrary to my expectations, he didn't seem surprised that I was writing a novel. Instead he told me in a voice that was less gruff than usual (even though it was irate, a fact I tried to ignore for the sake of my project): 'Of course, Farfar. You have every right to proceed as you please. Write about me and write about this beautiful aunt of yours. Write about that depraved environment you used to work in. I agree. Give me a piece of paper so I can write out my consent for you.' Yelling at my aunt, he added, 'Fetch a piece of paper and a pen, please . . . now.'

There was no need for her to rise panic-stricken, because I pulled out a sheet of my yellow paper and my Parker pen for him so he could write whatever he wanted.

The novel *A Moment of Love*, or *The Grub of Love* as I thought of it – although I would not have said that in public – by the new writer S. had recently been released by an impoverished local publisher with a subvention from the author, and a signing party for her was held in an unpretentious venue called Rasha Hall, which we kept under constant surveillance because of the questionable activities that took place there. That was outside my line of work, because for the most part I was far removed from the culture beat during my career, but this much I did know.

S. sat at a table piled with copies of the book, and I watched an unusual mix of people of all ages crowd around her. Each one purchased his copy and obtained the author's signature and a photo with the author; these were taken by the young man who at the Qasr al-Jummayz always held two books, one massive tome and one tiny leaflet. I had never bothered to learn his name. S. wasn't wearing her usual faded jeans. Instead she sported a green skirt and a white cotton blouse, and her black head cloth was held in place by multiple bobby pins to prevent it from falling and revealing her hair. No doubt this was a public relations ploy and a type of modesty adopted temporarily for the sake of the journalists who would cover the book launch. *This girl merits a lot of attention from my colleagues who remain in the service; there's no doubt about that.*

The jealousy I felt that day was painfully real when I saw the novel A.T. had called a larva offered for sale as a fully developed insect thanks to the advantage that beauty confers. All I had ever written had been 'The Apple', a security report that had blown my cover. I had read two of the books I had acquired from A'laf and felt that I could write something like them. Even so, I had written nothing. I listened to the cautious remarks that A.T. made at the reception; he spoke of the craft of writing, encouraging the writer S. without extolling her novel. He had written approximately the same comments in his preface for her book. When I listened to him, I felt devastated; I accepted my signed copy quickly and left that hall, heading straight for my yellow paper. I removed my vile leg and stripped off all my clothes. Then I sat in the nude to review the story of al-Mudallik, my aunt's spouse, and write it up. Perhaps the ritual of nudity would provide me with a grub that would develop; I didn't know.

When I finished reading to A.T. I was exhausted and

dripping with sweat. I glanced up at the novelist, trying to decipher his expression and detect either admiration or censure for the beginning of my novel, especially since he hadn't interrupted me this time; he had made me continue reading to the end. He seemed to be listening. Al-Bi'r Coffeehouse was almost empty at that hour of the day, and its proprietor, who could be seen either as a victim or a victimiser, was fiddling with his huge ring that contained a green turquoise, removing it and putting it back on his finger non-stop as the look in his eyes became reptilian. The coffeehouse's only waiter was slumped in a broken chair with rope webbing. He was half asleep, and an African woman in her early thirties was gazing at a number of pictures she had removed from her cloth handbag. She was weeping silently.

'So, Master, what do you think? Is this another dead grub?' I asked after a number of minutes had elapsed without the novelist saying anything. I guessed he was giving more thought to the African woman than to my first chapter. The woman, who was weeping over the photos, must provide some inspiration for him.

He replied, 'Of course it's a grub, Farfar, but it's not dead yet.'

My heart pounded. 'What do you mean?'

'You stuck to al-Mudallik's story literally – it's the story he told you. You haven't added any imaginative elements to it. He grew up in a deprived environment, but you don't flesh that out. It contained items of clothing, hurt feelings, jealousy, struggles, breakdowns, and other stuff. The mother sells yoghurt, but you write nothing about the source of milk in this poor household. Did she steal it or milk a hungry goat? Al-Mudallik hated his father because he was a tyrant; well, brother, what father doesn't seem tyrannical to his children – even mine or yours? Do you treat any consequences of this hatred in your novel? When does he rip apart his father's favourite shirt, for example? Does he destroy some of his father's produce? Does he conspire with other boys to put a big rock in front of the donkey that pulls the vegetable cart? You don't mention whether a donkey pulls the cart, but I doubt that the father used a Toyota or Mercedes truck – that's right, isn't it? You served the food too soon – before it was completely cooked. If you go home and put it back on the fire for a time, it may cook 'til it's done and perhaps the larva won't die.'

This was an extremely significant comment, but all the same I felt enraged. I thought it was really strange that in such a short time I should have become a preoccupation of this writer. Many people consider him a supercilious star who doesn't make friends easily. That was what I had thought too when I saw him for the first time in Qasr al-Jummayz talking about his eccentric rituals for writing. I had imagined that his face looked like a she-camel's – I don't know why that animal in particular. *It's true that I have appropriated these same rituals and have tried to implement them. The strange thing is that I'm very close to him. Why haven't the people who knew him before me, the ones who always sit with him, grown as close to him as I have? I'll return to the fire again, using the same nude writing ritual in a room without a breath of air. I'll make some changes to prevent the larva from dying. I'll invent quite a different childhood for al-Mudallik in the city of Sinka and see what my imagination, which has no doubt expanded, produces. For a novice, I've read an acceptable number of books. I've read The Residents of the Sa'd District Under Occupation, which he wrote in prison. I really liked it, even though it's not at all like the novel Eva. His Sa'd District is easy to read and discusses a group of Asian workers – their numbers have increased in the country recently – as they try to muddle their way through life in a poor neighbourhood called the Sa'd District, courting its women and hunting its cats and dogs, which district residents say they cook and serve for dinner. The novel is filled with ironic and endearing distinctions.*

The novelist seemed almost to have been reading my thoughts as I brooded about his interest in me, because suddenly he said, 'Don't be surprised about my interest in you, Farfar. I really like your will to change from the life you were living. I'll help you so you don't go back to writing security reports again. This is part of my mission in life, and I won't abandon it until I die.'

'Do you believe that I'll eventually succeed in writing about al-Mudallik in a top-notch fashion?'

'Of course you will. Al-Mudallik and the gravedigger and dozens of other stories and experiences that exist in your mind . . . that will all take a lot of effort to bring forth. Let me tell you about this woman who is weeping over those pictures – based on my imagination naturally, since I don't know anything about her.'

The African woman was now examining one of the pictures with even greater interest. She had placed it on the table in front of her after dusting it off very carefully with a tissue. The other photos she had put back in her cloth bag, from which she now brought out a tube of lipstick, an eyebrow pencil, and a black comb with some broken teeth and tufts of hair. She wiped her tears away with a dirty red handkerchief and then began to freshen up, combing her hair and using all the items she had taken from her bag. We watched her stealthily. The sole waiter was slumped over in the chair with rope webbing. The coffeehouse's proprietor had ceased toying with the ring and had risen to go out to the street. The novelist spoke as if dictating a novel; I was stunned by his brilliance and was painfully aware of my own shortcomings. After spending a considerable amount of time in cultured circles, I was still Farfar, the grub hunter.

'"I know you haven't died. My heart, which you have repeatedly tested and which you have always found to be true, tells me this. You haven't died. It's true that you joined the rebels and deserted a city that elicited a shriek from you when you saw it for the first time while we were landing in a small Fokker aircraft that brought us from the south: 'This is my city! This is my city!' Then you later returned south a fiery malcontent, tramping through forests where you cannot remember our love. But you're still alive. I sit now in a silent coffeehouse that lacks any soul. An exhausted waiter dozes in a chair. An old man who must be the coffeehouse's owner resembles an aged crone. Two strange men – one with a wooden leg – are speaking in whispers. They must be former school or prison buddies who have met by chance and are recalling some common memories. Your last photo is in front of me; an itinerant photographer took it in a garden where we were strolling. It's just a picture, but that's not what it seems to me. No, it's you in person, and I'm making myself pretty for it now. I'm applying my kohl and lipstick. I'm tracing my eyebrows and combing my hair, confident that you will rise from the table and embrace me. A number of your old friends visited me yesterday – men who served in the infantry with you. They are stern, gruff soldiers but they entered my house in civilian garb and displayed emotions that are typically human. You served with them and were stern when with them but delicate and gentle with me. I'll wait for you. Come back, I beg you. Rise from the table. Salute the two strangers whispering together about their memories. Rouse the slumped-over waiter; tell him to bring you tea with five spoons of sugar – the way you always love it.'"

*That's a strong opening, A.T... no doubt, very strong. Imagination has rescued what is actually a small sliver of reality, transforming it into a rich text. A weeping woman who adorns herself while looking at a photo in a filthy coffeehouse becomes a lover waiting for her true love, who has left her and fled to the south, rebelling against the regime; but she hasn't given up waiting for him. The difference between us is enormous. You're a trained professional, and I'm a novice. One is an imago hunter and the other a grub hunter. But I'll never admit defeat. I'll continue groping about with what I've begun 'til I become like you, A.T. I don't want to ask about your beginnings when you gave up teaching middle-school maths to write. Your first efforts must have been much stronger than mine since you left teaching for them. Unlike you, I'm a person whose profession abandoned him, a man who by chance learned that people without any prior relationship with writing have become writers. Then the crazy idea obsessed him that he should become one of them.*

*Chapter Fourteen*

*The Death of a Dolt* is the title of the second play I attended at the urging of al-Mudallik, who came to my house three times in one week, interrupting my reading and writing, to remind me of the time of the Civic Youth Theatre performance of this play. His role in it is actually no more than a walk-on part for an extra. There was really no need for al-Mudallik to be so insistent, since I intended to attend the play voluntarily, because exploring his character has become a pressing concern for me. I rewrote my beginning, which is about him, and felt greatly relieved. A.T. would no doubt like it when I presented it to him at al-Bi'r Coffeehouse. Imagination figures in it – I'm sure of that. I invented elements for it that al-Mudallik hadn't told me. I also attempted to imitate A.T.'s use of language.

There wasn't much of a crowd in front of the theatre – nothing to compare with the mobs at the stadium near my house. There was no pushing or shoving, no yelling, and no vendors scattered here and there selling lupin seeds or drinks. The people who had turned out for the play were a dapper bunch, and each person waited in the queue for his turn at the ticket window. There he quietly purchased his ticket and entered the theatre. Al-Mudallik was waiting for me at the side door, where VIP patrons entered. His clothes were very ordinary – black trousers and a white shirt – and no medal hung from his neck. I was severely tempted to search his pockets for poison or tranquillisers but remembered that his part didn't involve any fainting this time. Aunt Th. was there too, smiling and elegant. She stood erect with no hint of a bent back. She was sedately dressed and wore the perfume she had brought from Dubai. She wanted to sit with me during the play, but I apologised to her gently, because I had agreed to sit with A.T., who was already seated, gazing anxiously at the curtain, which was still closed. I saw the newly minted novelist S., who had reverted to faded jeans and the silk scarf that would slip to reveal her hair. She wasn't in the orchestra section this time and wasn't seated near the novelist. She was six rows back, and a young man with tousled hair sat beside her. He held a large notebook, and there was a blue pencil behind his ear. He looked like one of those journalists who hover around culture but lack talent. S. was no doubt a success; she had successfully produced what would still be a grub if I, Abdullah Farfar – or one of those other idiots who fill coffeehouses with chatter and cigarette smoke – had written it, thanks to beauty's unfair advantage. In my opinion, though, she wasn't beautiful, not even close; she seemed to have thumbed her nose at this advantage. She was off in the distance, and the young man was whispering to her. I watched her chest rise and fall as she, doubtless, inhaled his praise.

The performance proceeded in a tedious, boring fashion. I know that performances at the Civic Youth Theatre are always boring. They call it 'experimental theatre', but I call it 'detrimental theatre'. Our security agency, no matter how hard it tries, cannot get charges to stick against this theatre's directors, who vilify the nation, disparage the homeland, comport themselves like tramps, and stick their tongues out, without anyone catching on. The dolt who was supposed to die at the end of the play and whom al-Mudallik, assisted by another extra, was to carry off stage, wore ragged clothes. He danced at times, sang at times, and recited poetry in a weepy voice. He stumbled into the women walking in front of him and collided with the men's shoulders. At one point he stood before a withered tree with the word 'freedom' inscribed on it. Then he laughed while standing in front of a building supply store. He fell in a hole and hit his head on a wooden post. At the end, a dapper man, who was pointing a gun at his face, asked, 'Are you the cricket that lives in the stubble patch? Are you my slave?' When he said, 'Yes', the man shot him. He fell to the ground, and the shooter walked away steadily. Next al-Mudallik and his mate entered with a torn litter on which they placed the corpse before carrying it offstage. The audience rose and applauded, expecting the curtain to close to announce the play's end. But it didn't close, and al-Mudallik returned to the stage once more, dragging the litter after him with the actor who had played the dolt still on it. Al-Mudallik stopped near the front of the stage, and the shrouded actor, who was no doubt astonished, lay silently in front of him.

Then al-Mudallik began to scream, in a voice I had never heard him use, pointing back and forth from the litter to the audience. 'Rest in peace, my son. Your blood won't have been shed in vain, because this is a country of justice, freedom, and democracy. It won't have been shed in vain when thousands of eyes watch over the nation's security. Thousands of extraordinary men protect the homeland and block traitors who would like to see the nation dismembered – such despicable traitors, such rubbish! Martyr, lie in peace! Rest in peace. Each of us will give his life for you. Each of us will give his life for the nation. Long live our faithful leaders! Down with communism! Down with imperialism! Down with America!'

I rose in alarm, feeling cramps at the bottom of my tummy. So this was the surprise that I had sensed would occur but had wanted to discount! All his insistence about inviting me to see a man enter and exit, without speaking a word – there had been something behind it. I heard a thunderous chant resound in the theatre. 'God is most great! Allahu Akbar! Down with the traitors! Down with imperialism! Down with America!' A large number of spectators shoved towards the stage. They lifted al-Mudallik on their shoulders and carried him out the theatre's main entrance. Then their chants gradually grew fainter as they marched away. The curtain was still open, and a large number of the play's actors along with its director came out on stage from behind the scenes. They were assessing the situation when the actor who had played the hero rose from his litter and began to gaze wide-eyed at the spectacle. Aunt Th., looking like a wax effigy, had remained seated throughout this whole row. The novelist A.T. left quickly without saying goodbye to me. Most of the other members of the intelligentsia in the orchestra section rushed away, their facial expressions ravaged by raw fear. I wasn't at all upset about the anarchy unleashed by al-Mudallik. To the contrary, I was really delighted, first because in my opinion al-Mudallik had just become a person of national significance, whereas I had always considered him a person of marginal importance – one of those we refer to in our security reports as 'hoi polloi'. Their files are placed in a cabinet set apart from those used in daily searches. Secondly, I was delighted because this character, which is my exclusive property, provides me with some new surprise every day – with a surprise that speeds up the cooking of my writing. Al-Mudallik's character is a treasure, as I've always said.

We learned subsequently that al-Mudallik had turned off the electric motor for the curtain to keep it from closing at the end of the play. He had screamed at the actor who played the dolt to rest quietly on his litter and not leave it. Then he had dragged him with uncanny speed back out on stage. We discovered that my aunt's husband had totally torpedoed the play *Death of a Dolt* at its premiere. The play had been meant as a critique of the ruling establishment. The doltish folks stumble down the streets, stand up, fall, dance, and sing, because there's nothing else left for them to do besides dance and sing. They weep over freedom, which has died, and laugh while looking at a building supply store, because it symbolises the kind of development that isn't conceivable for the likes of them. Then their representative is dispatched by the cold lead of a government-issue bullet. Foreign aid arrives to find him dead and being carried away on a litter for burial. The director, A.J., was one of the most important directors of experimental youth theatre and had racked up a huge dossier in our agency where he is known as a destructive leftist. He tugged at his hair in despair after witnessing his critical text subverted at the end into a major demonstration in support of the regime.

I took my aunt, who was still in shock, home to my house for the time being. The impact that Dubai had made on her and that had followed her back here suddenly dissipated, to be replaced by the shock of seeing her husband borne off on people's shoulders in a night-time demonstration, which I followed on my mobile phone, because from one moment to the next I was in touch with some of my former National Security colleagues who were keeping tabs on the demonstration to prevent it from being infiltrated by destructive elements – as typically happens in these instances.

Al-Mudallik came to my house with the first strands of dawn's light, searching for his wife. He was reeling from exhaustion, his throat was parched, and his neck was bereft of medals. He asked for supper and a cigarette but dozed off in his chair before he could eat or smoke. My aunt was also slumbering in a chair, but I was almost incandescent I was so alert. I trashed my revised beginning and sat down, without employing any special ritual, to write a new one. My beginning started where the story should end – from al-Mudallik's voice on stage, from the moment he had, quite simply, demolished a theatrical idea that had quite possibly taken a long time for someone to write and direct. When he woke up, he would ask me what I thought of his performance. I would be candid with him, belittling the role of the litter bearer and lauding the other role – not that of the madman who gave a speech that turned into a demonstration – but the role of someone who possessed a treasure that would transform my writing.

*Chapter Fifteen*

The novelist A.T. wasn't at al-Bi'r Coffeehouse, where I would usually meet him early in the day. We would sit by ourselves and talk about my larvae and his fully grown insects before I would accompany him – or he would go alone – to meet his other friends at Qasr al-Jummayz. His mobile phone was turned off all yesterday, and I thought he was either sick or had begun writing a new novel for which he was wandering the streets, closeted in his room, in prison, or renting some nasty zar house to compose it. Perhaps, as he had previously suggested, he was writing about the impoverished football player who had become a government minister or perhaps his new novel began with the story he had improvised about the African woman who was weeping in al-Bi'r Coffeehouse. He had liked it and had wanted to finish it as part of some new project. I knew he went crazy when writing; perhaps he had boarded a military aircraft for battlefields in the south to research the novel. I had learned this from listening to him and from watching him while he improvised the long paragraph about the woman I saw weeping there that day. His eyes had been flashing insanely.

Yesterday at noon when al-Mudallik awoke from his slumbers in my house, rubbed his eyes, and observed stacked on the table more than ten pieces of yellow paper covered with writing, he laughed because he realised that he had inspired me to write something. He didn't pick up any of the pieces of paper but took his four medals from his pocket. Three were for *Perfumed Sealing Wax*, the fourth did not say *The Death of a Dolt* but *The Life of a Martyr*. So al-Mudallik had been planning that tumultuous demonstration for some time and had taken its plans to Dubai to be recorded in an artistically wrought medal. He hung his four medals on his chest and turned towards me, eyes sparkling brilliantly. 'I trounced the traitors, Farfar. Isn't that so?'

'But you also trounced your acting career. No one will offer you another part in a play.'

'Says who?'

He moved suddenly, shaking the medals on his chest vigorously.

'Says who?' he asked again. 'Yesterday the entire nation carried me on their shoulders, and the sales manager for the soft drinks firm Nani offered me a role in an ad for his drinks. I've finally made it to television. I've made it to TV. Rise, woman, and hear the news. Get up.'

He shook my aunt, who was curled up in a chair, snoring intermittently. He struck the table with his other hand, making the pages of my manuscript jump. What I witnessed next was weird: my aunt rose with an agility that suggested none of the stiffness of age nor her torpor of the previous day and embraced him vigorously. They were clinging to each other as they left my house. I heard my aunt say in a sleepy voice, 'We'll go to Dubai again – won't we?'

Al-Bi'r Coffeehouse was different today. Totally missing were the men of the desert and the country bumpkins who relaxed there while raiding the city. Instead, I saw that most or almost all of its tables were occupied by southern Sudanese who lived in the capital. They wore African garments adorned with red, yellow, and lavender and held flags that differed radically from the nation's. A large portrait of their most famous leader, who had recently died in a tragic accident, was prominently displayed at the front of the coffeehouse where everyone who entered would see it. He was dressed in the same bright African garb. His head sported a palm leaf hat with a rooster feather in the centre.

I asked the coffeehouse's proprietor about this suspicious gathering as he flitted agilely between the tables, assisting his only waiter. His tunic raised to his navel, he replied in his old lady's voice, 'They're commemorating the anniversary of their leader.

Where's your friend Satan?'

I don't know why Satan was the name he chose for the novelist, whom I had once imagined as a she-camel; I had never thought A.T. resembled Satan, although I don't know what Satan looks like. I ignored this comment and asked, 'Why are they holding the commemoration here? Is this a place where commemorations are held?'

I was speaking rather loudly – I don't know why – and was about to curse him and his tribe, even though I didn't know which it was, when I noticed that his face was drowning in kohl, his tunic was hiked up to his belly button, and his ring was gleaming provocatively. He in no way looked like a victim – as A.T. had imagined; instead, he was a hard-boiled victimiser, who would stop at nothing.

'I unite hearts, Woody. I unite divergent factions. Return tomorrow and you'll find a table here for you and your friend Satan. Today my cuisine is entirely southern.'

He laughed, but this was a serpent's hiss. The hand he suddenly extended to touch my wooden leg had traces of henna designs on it.

The sky was cloudy when I returned to the street, and I could discern the smell of distant rain. A number of Toyota Land Cruisers with distinctive plates and heavily tinted glass were parked nearby. My former colleagues were, no doubt, observing the leader's remembrance at close range. They wouldn't allow it to develop into anything more than a commemoration.

By the time I reached Qasr al-Jummayz, I had exhausted both my despicable leg and my sound one. I had to stop a number of times and feel them before I resumed my walk. In my pocket I had my entire first chapter about al-Mudallik and was keen to show it to the novelist A.T. so I could hear his opinion, which would most likely be encouraging and supportive, but he wasn't there either. S. was sitting at A.T.'s table – or rather a new version of S. now that her novel, *A Moment of Love* or *The Grub of Love* as I thought of it, had been released. Around her were new faces I had never seen before except for the young man with tousled hair I had seen with her at the Civic Youth Theatre. The familiar faces I always saw were at a different table. S. seemed to be engaged in an interview, because the guy with tousled hair was writing in his notebook.

She interrupted her remarks when she saw me hobble into the coffeehouse and called to me in a voice that also sounded new but had a malicious ring. 'Come here, Abdullah . . . Have you finished *A Moment of Love*? Your opinion matters to me.'

She didn't say 'Farfar' and she was requesting my valuable opinion. I hadn't read her novel and never would, because I feared it would ruin my writing and that I might find myself penning phrases like 'Refrain from massaging my feelings, O Masseur, spouse of my aunt. My feelings, like my wooden leg, do not respond to blandishments.' I laughed to myself as I reviewed my sentences, which meant nothing – exactly like her grub, which was also meaningless. *I will flatter her; it doesn't matter. I know full well that she cares nothing for me or my opinion. She's actually furious at me because recently I've come nearer to her former shining star than she has. In the past, she used to sit so close to him she was almost inside his ribcage.*

'I actually haven't finished it yet, but the opening is engaging. I'm busy writing a novel.'

'Is that true, Abdullah? Congrats! A thousand congrats!'

All at once she bubbled with phony delight. I knew her glee wasn't related to my writing but no doubt to a larva of love she fondled with her hands like a valued trinket while talking with me. 'What's your novel about, Friend? Don't tell me it's a love story too?'

She was doubtless making fun of me. I had frightened her with my wooden leg, and the first day I saw her I had pointed out that I had made some stabs at writing. I have learned from hanging out with these types that people who attempt to write are in their eyes nothing more than triflers with nothing to show – people who come to flirt with one of them or to drink coffee on someone else's tab before heading out. *Fine, Ms Faded-Blue-Jeans – who temporarily wore conservative clothes as a public relations ploy at her book-signing – very soon you'll see a novel just as good as A.T.'s. You'll learn about al-Mudallik, whose cry frightened you, causing you to flee from the theatre leaning on the arm of your journalist friend with tousled hair. You'll find that it's written with an amount of imagination that you'll never be able to copy.* I didn't answer her question; instead I asked about the novelist A.T. She didn't know where he was. On hearing my question, one of the writer's friends at the other table said the master was taking a break from the coffee-house and his friends to write a new novel inspired by an astonishing personality – one of a type rarely encountered.

He had postponed writing the football player novel he had been planning. 'He told me: "Explain my absence to my friends."'

I felt genuinely frustrated. I thought it odd that he had disappeared without telling me, because I consider myself his closest friend and pupil, someone who listens carefully to his advice and follows his opinions and rituals. My first chapter, which I had with me, sprang from my meetings with him. It was about a personality I had discussed with him so frequently that he had learned everything about it. He had seen this character come vibrantly alive on stage. I suddenly trembled violently and sensed that I was about to fall. It was obvious that the novelist had stolen the character of al-Mudallik from me. Damn! He had stolen it. He had stolen my character and disappeared to write the novel sitting naked now in a room without a breath of air or roaming through neighbourhoods and down alleys I don't know or he's in prison, in various stadia, or in the house of Ammuna the Ethiopian. He may have boarded a filthy bus for the city of Sinka in the east to live in poverty there for several days to connect with al-Mudallik's childhood. I had been a fool to tell him all that. I felt that the scheme on which I had laboured so hard for all this time was about to implode. Who would read a novel that Abdullah Farfar wrote about a character A.T. had already written about? People would say, 'A ridiculous imitation.' They would refer to it as theft and child's play. They would say . . . My head was ringing; my ears were ringing. I couldn't feel my vile leg. I heard someone say, 'He's drunk.' Another person suggested, 'High blood pressure . . . severe intestinal cramps. Call an ambulance.' I watched the spectral figure of S. speak excitedly on her mobile phone.

When I regained consciousness in the hospital, the doctors told me that I had no real medical illness. They tested my blood and examined my vital functions – heart to kidneys – without discovering anything. 'It's simply a nervous collapse, and the symptoms will gradually subside, Abdullah. You'll be able to resume your normal routine. You must have suffered some shock.'

I hadn't been totally unconscious; I had been dreaming. I had dreamt I was riding a roiling wave in a lavender sea. I held a book called *Four Medals and al-Mudallik*. The cover picture was the southern leader wearing a colourful rooster feather on his head. Suddenly from the far side of the sea, a person with a flaming face and wooden ears appeared; he told me he was the novelist Satan and attempted to wrest the book from my hand while I tried to prevent him. Together we sank into the lavender sea.

With the journalist who had tousled hair and some others in tow, the novelist S. came to reassure herself that I was still alive. She brought another copy of *The Grub of Love* to provide me with entertaining reading for my convalescence. Many other patrons of Qasr al-Jummayz came, if only out of curiosity. I was astounded by the presence beside me of Aunt Th. and her husband, al-Mudallik. I had no idea how they had learned about my great fall, which had happened far from their house. The real surprise, though, was when I saw the proprietor of al-Bi'r Coffeehouse enter my room bearing a basket of fruit. He yelled, 'Get well, Woody! Just a passing crisis, Woody.'

*Four Medals and al-Mudallik* – I pounded my head in rage. This title had come to me when I was in a coma and had subsequently stuck in my memory even when I came to. It was a super name even though it had arrived too late, after the central character of my novel had been lost. All the same I felt a kind of bliss. I had definitely progressed, even if there was not much daylight between *The Failed Thespian* and *Four Medals and al-Mudallik*. I sensed that I had acquired some culture. The prime indicator of my progress was my persistence in writing. *I'll write in my own way even if I never publish my novel and if A. T. does publish his. I could recruit a number of former colleagues to search for A. T. in every square foot he might occupy. They would take him where he would fall to his hands and knees to beg for a cigarette. They would do it, but no . . . No, this grub writer is far removed from the former writer of police reports.*

I suddenly remembered another personality I hadn't told the novelist A.T. much about. I had not discussed this other character because I hadn't studied him as carefully as al-Mudallik. This character would no doubt help me. I would work on him in complete secrecy, putting him cheek by jowl with al-Mudallik to see what developed. At this point I decided to visit the cheerleader-gravedigger in al-Qasr al-Abyad just as soon as my wooden leg was able to support me again.

I searched for my mobile phone and after several attempts eventually found it in the hospital's cloakroom for personal effects. I rang A.T.'s number and heard a recorded message: 'This subscriber is unavailable at present. Try the number again later. Thank you.'

*Chapter Sixteen*

At the door of al-Qasr al-Abyad, or 'The White Castle', the largest hospital for mental illnesses in the capital, the doorman – whose clothing and rugged features suggested that he was a northerner – scrutinised my wooden leg and informed me that no visits were allowed at this time. If I planned to enter the building, I would need to return in the afternoon. I didn't quarrel with him. Instead I searched my pockets for my old Security Services ID. It was still valid, since it hadn't been considered a perquisite that the agency needed to reclaim – unlike my weapon and walkie-talkie. I hadn't actually carried the card deliberately after I left the service and began knocking on writing's door. It had simply leapt into my pockets out of force of habit whenever I changed clothes. I discovered it in its normal place in my shirt pocket and swiped it past the eyes of the doorman, who trembled and raised his hand in a ridiculous attempt at a military salute. He did not merely open the entrance door; he left his guard post and escorted me into the building. He kept repeating, 'Step this way, Your Honour . . . at your service, Your Honour.'

In a ward called the Sulayman Ward, which had been named for one of the late founders of the hospital and which was reserved for the severest cases, I found the cheerleading gravedigger A.D. and felt glum. I wasn't surprised to feel sad, because this was, no doubt, part and parcel of my new metamorphosis: a onetime author of police reports who had evolved into an author of grubs. A.D. was oblivious to the world, staring up at the ceiling from which the paint was peeling; flakes of it fell on his bed. His clothing, which wasn't Sufi green as in the past, was made of a light, white fabric that revealed how emaciated his body was now. It was the body of an aged boy. Seated next to him on the bed was a woman with a sorrowful face. I deduced that she was his wife; I knew he was married and had children. The newspaper clippings with his photos from the reception honouring him were arranged on the table beside him, and the edges of some of them were damp. The woman rose when she saw me hobble up beside her. She wasn't put off by my vile leg; she was in a place more wretched than any wooden leg.

Looking off into the distance, she asked, 'Do you know my husband? I haven't seen you before.'

She asked me this because women in our country know their husbands' acquaintances, regardless of whether the friend has frequented their home. A wife and children know all about any friends of the master of the house.

'When we were young we worked at the same sauce

factory and as adults we have both been cheerleaders for athletic clubs – him for al-Lablab and me for al-Marid.'

Half of my claim was fabricated. The factual part was that the cheerleader-gravedigger had worked as a porter for a sauce plant when he was young. I don't know where it was located or whether it is still in operation. I had unearthed this piece of information after a day of investigation. The team called al-Marid, or 'The Rebel', for which I claimed to be a cheerleader, was actually the team that employed al-Mudallik, my aunt's husband. I had no tie to any athletic team except that their matches were held near my house.

'Look at him . . . You've got to help him.'

She was weeping, and I sensed that I was becoming emotional too. If I write about the cheerleading gravedigger, I will write in a sorrowful, humane way. During this hospitalisation, although he was oblivious to his surroundings, he was encircled by photos of the recognition that had cost him his mind and almost killed him. He was an inspiration to me, and this tragedy's inspiration was very evident, both in that location and in my mind. Which ritual of the traitorous novelist, who had stolen my character al-Mudallik, would suit this tragedy do you suppose? Would it be ritual elegance – writing in a swanky hotel lobby while attired in my suit that had been altered by the tailor Kh.R.? The naked ritual in a room devoid of even a breath of air? The ritual of roaming the streets and digging graves? The novelist had never said anything about writing in a hospital he had entered with bogus symptoms, or in a cemetery where he dug a grave and lay in it while writing. I could do that, and it would be my ritual for writing about the scrawny cheerleader-gravedigger who lay as if dead in the Sulayman Ward. Who do you suppose will dig his grave?

His wife snatched my train of thought and told me that her husband's friends had found a grave that was already dug in the Umran Cemetery where he had worked. It had two gravestones on which his name and date of birth were carved. The death date would be left blank until he died. He had dug his own grave then. Perhaps that was the last grave he ever dug before losing his mind. Today I'll write the cheerleader's story. I'll write it today, ignoring the shock and breakdown I experienced. When the novelist A.T. returns – delighted with his new, plagiarised novel – he will find that I have a different novel no one knows anything about. Without paying attention to what I was doing, I brought out my mobile phone and dialled the number that obsessed me whenever I wasn't thinking about writing. Then I heard the same recording: 'This subscriber cannot be reached at the present time.'

I took some money from my wallet and placed it in front of the woman. Then I left al-Qasr al-Abyad without offering to help her husband. This mental hospital is in a suburb surrounded by parched land, very far from the centre of the capital. I found a taxi only with enormous difficulty. The first two drivers were slick operators who apparently judge the folks who try to flag them down by their clothes. They no doubt took one look at my vile leg and decided not to stop. The driver who finally did pick me up wasn't really the taxi driver that his passengers thought he was. He was one of my former colleagues, one of a group of recruits I once trained to set aside their feelings. As he was driving me to Qasr al-Jummayz at my request, he told me that a file had recently been opened for me at the agency, and that he himself had done that. It wasn't about Abdullah Harfash, the former agent, as a preparation for his return to the force, but in my new character as a suspicious literary fellow who must be tracked carefully.

He warned me, 'Watch out, Uncle Farfar. I'm telling you on account of the time we spent together and the bread and salt we've shared.'

I could have laughed as I imagined myself a suspect shadowed by our security agencies after I had spent my entire life pursuing suspects until that unforeseen accident at the farm we had under surveillance. What made me want to laugh the most was that I had yet to produce anything that could be studied for subversive tendencies.

At Qasr al-Jummayz, none of the coterie was present, even though it was the time they usually met. One of the Ethiopian waitresses told me in her alluring broken Arabic that they had been there earlier and had left for the party. I didn't know what party she meant – some book-signing? I couldn't think of any book that a member of the group had released which justified a party. S. had held hers at

Rasha Hall, and that was finished. I sat at my table alone and ordered a coffee without any sugar. Then I began observing the coffeehouse's hubbub. A man wearing a tunic and a turban looked around apprehensively. I easily recognised him as a former colleague, although an inexperienced one. No doubt he was trailing someone in the coffeehouse, perhaps me. Two foreign ladies – possibly from Europe or America – decked out in many locally made accessories that were made of beads and ivory, were trying to speak Arabic and asked the waitress to bring them some incense called *al-qard*. It is reputed in our culture to ward off the evil eye and other forms of envy but isn't one of the forms of incense stocked by Qasr al-Jummayz. I was thinking about al-Mudallik and the gravedigger at the same time. One man was teeming with life while the other was slipping toward death. *Why not write about both of them? Why not mix them together in a complicated text that would intimidate A. T. when he returned, leaving his plagiarised text behind in the mud. He would kiss my head and give me back the character of al-Mudallik with esteem and honour.* I smiled to myself. My imagination had no doubt begun to expand. It had expanded even more than was necessary.

*Chapter Seventeen*

On my way through the Umran Cemetery, where the cheerleader had once been a gravedigger and where he now lay in a grave he had dug himself before expiring, I stopped numerous times to wipe the sweat from my face and to jot down some preliminary observations for my novel on the yellow paper that I always carry in my pocket.

The cemetery is ancient and far from my house. I reached it in a motorised rickshaw and asked the driver to wait for me until I returned; I wasn't sure that he would. The many modern buildings that had been built near the cemetery caught my eye. I hadn't visited this cemetery since my mother was buried there more than fifteen years earlier. The most striking of these new structures was a white, two-storey building on a large tract of land. Over its low wall and through the gaps between the green trees lining this wall, I could see a large number of children playing ball, gleefully racing each other, or swinging in the rope swings that were scattered through the garden. Women dressed in white circulated among the children, and their cries mixed with the kids' yells. The large door that directly faced the cemetery bore no sign, but with a little effort I was able to deduce that it was a shelter for foundlings that had recently been established with funds contributed by some benefactors inside and outside the country. This was a home for children born out of wedlock, kids raised on the street, on top of dumpsters, or on the roofs of deserted houses – children their deadbeat parents had abandoned. Our agency didn't bother with social concerns like these that weren't related to national security.

I would not have had any reason to visit here had A.D. not died in the Sulayman Ward of The White Castle. He was now my character, and I had written a large part of his story from my imagination, mixing it with my imaginative biography of al-Mudallik, my aunt's husband. I was holding it for the return of the treasonous novelist. Then I would zap him when he read what I had written. I did not bear him any grudge or hatred and believed that his treachery had goaded me and made me hunch over my paper for many nights.

It had been fifteen days since the novelist disappeared, and I had kept dialling his number from my phone. I would not hang up until the boring recorded message ended with: 'Try again.' I had, time after time. I went to his house one day and pounded on the door almost as forcefully as when I pursued traitors and tracked them to some lair. To my astonishment the door opened, but this wasn't the novelist. This was another, younger man who looked like the novelist. I learned that he was the novelist's brother who lived in a provincial city in the west of the country. He came to the capital from time to time to visit his brother and had a house key to use when he came. He knew nothing about his brother's disappearance but wasn't alarmed.

He said, 'He's definitely writing somewhere. That's not a problem. There's nothing to worry about from his point of view, but it's a big problem for me.'

During those fifteen days I went to Qasr al-Jummayz a number of times and mingled with the novelist S. and her new set, which formed after she published her book. Under intense pressure from her, I revealed to her the topic of the novel I'm writing. I told her it's about the planet Mars where I think intelligent life exists and where the creatures are threatened by lethal floods and whirlwinds. I had constructed a novel from those assumptions.

'I didn't know you had such a vast imagination,' she said, without lifting a finger to adjust her silk scarf, which had fallen, revealing her hair, which had been bleached in a tasteless fashion that in no way made her look like a blonde. One of the men sitting with her read in a hushed voice an excerpt from *A Moment of Love* and then shouted, 'My God, you're really a genius!' The rash girl had trod with all her weight on a hornet's nest, and her file was definitely growing fatter at our agency.

I returned as well to al-Bi'r Coffeehouse, hoping fervently that I would find A.T. sitting there and that the startling character he had written about would be the victim who ran the coffeehouse – especially because he had written about a similar figure in his novel *The Residents of the Sa'd District Under Occupation* and in another novel that I hadn't read yet but that I had purchased from the A'laf Bookstore together with the other books that formed the nucleus of my library. But he also was not there.

I poked my head through the door and quickly withdrew it when I heard the effeminate voice of the coffeehouse's proprietor call to me, 'Come in, Woody. Have you recovered and been released? Come in. Today my cuisine is cosmopolitan.'

He was telling the truth about that, because when I had poked my head inside I had seen dozens of different miens that represented dozens of tribes and ethnic groups. I was going to look back inside and ask if he had seen Satan during the last few days, but his voice reached me: 'Where is Satan, Woody? Has he died in the fire?'

I felt even more incredulous. *Why Satan?*

The advertisement for the soft drinks company Nani had been filmed recently, produced with a speed I found astonishing. I was forced to watch it when it premiered on the local TV station. I found al-Mudallik, accompanied by my aunt, hammering on my door. They entered without a word, carrying a pack of Nani drinks they placed on my table. Then al-Mudallik headed straight for my dust-covered television, which I had forgotten for some time and neglected in my inner room along with a number of other items I wasn't using. He dusted it off thoroughly, brought it back to the living room, and plugged it in. Then he turned to the local station and lit a cigarette.

'Drink Nani and grow young again. Drink Nani and savour life's taste.'

In the ad, al-Mudallik was an old man leaning on a brown stick. He held a red bottle and sipped slowly from it while taking deep breaths. Then, in another scene, he appeared with dyed hair and his chest puffed out. He was wearing youthful attire and stood on a crowded street corner where he flirted with schoolgirls, who smiled back at him.

'You know, Farfar – there's a lot of truth to these ads. I sense that the fizz of youth has returned since I began drinking Nani on a regular basis. Ask your aunt if you don't believe it. Have some. Try it.'

He held a bottle out to me after opening it with his teeth; that feat had caused some drops to spill on his clothes. I drank it meekly but didn't sense anything except that the taste of the mint extract made me feel sick to my stomach. I noticed that my aunt was covering her face with the end of her *thawb* out of embarrassment and that henna had, it seemed, been quite liberally applied to her hands and feet. *Damn you, Uncle! Damn you, my aunt's husband – why were you stolen from me like this?*

'Did they pay you a lot for this advertisement?'

I asked that, expecting to hear he hadn't received any recompense. I didn't think it was a catchy ad, because people are accustomed to seeing attractive faces in ads, faces that entice a person to buy the product. But al-Mudallik surprised me. He stretched a hand out to a woman's handbag that hung from my aunt's shoulder, even though I had never seen her carry a handbag before. Opening it, he extracted two tickets sporting the Etihad Airways logo.

Waving these in my face, he said, 'Don't forget to write about this in your story.'


When I finally found the cheerleader's grave, I sat down beside it and recited the Fatiha for his spirit. His grave was surrounded by other ones, and I read the names of their occupants. They sounded familiar to me – names I had heard before. Perhaps they had been well-known politicians who had once ruled the country, singers who had filled the world with jubilant noise and then departed, or football players from the community among whom the cheerleader-gravedigger had lived for a long time, loving it and dying for it. I took one of my pieces of yellow paper from my pocket to record my observations, which – after I reread them several times – I decided were good enough to include in the novel.

I wrote: 'When I gazed at his grave at an hour when the Sun seemed in a hurry to set to leave the stage for night, it did not appear to me that I was looking at a dry pit that held a body devoid of a spirit. Instead, this was a fragrant chamber; perfumed with incense, it held a bridegroom who would be escorted to his wedding that evening. I remembered his powerful voice that had rocked stadiums with a mighty cheer and his strong hands that had pulverised the earth until dirt fled in alarm.'

A. T., these lines have some imagination in them, don't they? You'll go crazy when you hear them, and there is a lot more.

*Chapter Eighteen*

One day I was practising ritual nudity and clad only in underpants, sitting in my room with the curtains drawn and not a breath of air stirring, writing on my yellow paper, adding touches and revising, when I heard my mobile phone ring; I had forgotten to turn it off. Usually I switch it off when I write and I also detach the vile leg from my body, casting it as far away as possible to make myself feel incapacitated and unlikely to move just because I feel bored.

It had been more than three weeks since the novelist A.T.'s disappearance. When I went to his house a second time, the door was opened by his brother, clad in wet underclothes, although a faded pink towel was wrapped around his head. Through the opening of the door, which he was trying to block with his body, I could see the silhouette of a half-naked woman moving about in the house's living room, but the novelist hadn't come out of hiding yet. Al-Mudallik and my aunt had travelled once more to Dubai, where they had spent three days in the Ghulum Ikhlasi Hotel, which al-Mudallik liked. He had told the travel agents for the Nani Soft Drinks firm about this hotel, and they had booked a room there for the couple. On their return, they visited my house to hand me my present. This time it was a more significant item. It was a Bati watch – I had never heard of this brand before – and it featured a black dial without any hands. I was obliged to put it on while al-Mudallik watched – after he yanked my old West End watch with the faded green dial from my wrist, yelling, 'Do you call what you have on a watch, Farfar? Toss this junk in the trash.'

He hurled it with such force that it smashed against the concrete blocks of the living room wall. Thanks to his impetuous outburst I lost a keepsake I cherished dearly. That watch had been my companion for half my life and could have spent the rest of it with me if it hadn't been destroyed. I yelled at him — the second or third time I had done that – but he paid no attention. He was talking about Dubai non-stop. 'Imagine, Farfar: they have refrigerated summer by using technology. They have imported ice from the ends of the Earth. Imagine this: they live in paradise. Do you know what paradise is? Don't be sad. I'll arrange a ticket for you on our next trip and a room in the Ghulum Hotel. My friend Ghulum, who is a fine fellow – can you imagine? – started as a beggar in the streets when he arrived from his country and rose to own a hotel through his wits. He told me that himself. It's true that his hotel doesn't have a star rating, but it's better than the Hilton. By God Almighty, it is better. Ask your aunt if you don't believe me. Ask her about the sheets, curtains, and the European bathroom.'

I quit yelling because he had vanquished me. He had incited me to keep writing the creation that I expected would not be just another grub this time. But where was the man who would listen to my larvae and judge them?

After it rang quite a few times – six or seven (my ringtone is from the old song 'My Life', which is my favorite song) – I answered my phone and trembled momentarily when I saw my former supervisor's number. I hadn't erased it when I erased the numbers of many of my former colleagues when they did not communicate with me or return my calls. Actually I felt scared every time I considered erasing it. Onerous training had instilled in me the idea that your boss remains your boss even if he dies or you die.

I pressed the button while trying to calm myself. Then I heard my boss ask sharply, 'Why didn't you answer my call immediately, Farfar? Come to my office at the agency at once. I think you remember where it is?'

I turned off the phone, feeling very nervous. Many months had passed since my leg had been amputated, I had been forced into retirement, and my metamorphosis had begun. I had not seen my supervisor since then except for the time I went to request the release of 'The Slaughtered Bird' (the treacherous novelist) from our dungeon, where he had spent three barren days that had dried up all his thinking, as he confided to me. Later, one of my colleagues, who was working undercover as a taxi driver, had told me that they had recently opened a file on me. I was scared, really scared, and felt hundreds of different emotions – actually thousands – even though in the past I had tracked people down without experiencing a thing. It would be impossible for me to return to the service with this galling leg. I would definitely be arrested; they would want me to turn myself in, to arrest myself. At that moment I cursed the Bengali florist and the female African immigrant who had inspired him to write a novel, the impoverished cobbler from Rwanda and his ill-omened war, and the forgettable prostitute who had dazzled readers with her two novels. I almost cursed al-Mudallik, my aunt's husband, and the late gravedigger for coming my way and for making me think that they were valuable characters – not to mention the novelist A.T. for making me read *Eva Died in My Bed*, *The Residents of the Sa'd District Under Occupation*, and many other stories. He had befriended me until the theft occurred and he ripped me off.

'What do you have against its author?' The Christian R.M., proprietor of the A'laf Bookstore, had asked me that when I bought *Eva*, and his question still echoed in my ears. I do not have anything against its author. I am out of the service. I am a writer, a master of stabs, but the agency certainly has things against him and against me and against the novelist S. – the author of *The Grub of Love* who usually wears faded jeans but dressed conservatively for her book-signing – and against everyone who sits in Qasr al-Jummayz and the other treasonous coffeehouses that are filled with scallywags and folks who dream up intrigues and conspiracies.

It took me two hours to reach my supervisor's office in the agency's building. Half this time was spent waiting by the road, searching for transport. For the other half of the time I was crammed into a mediocre bus that is part of the public bus system. No one had the grace to rise and give me his seat, even though I hiked up my tunic so my wooden leg would show clearly.

I found him seated calmly behind his desk, and he welcomed me with a smile that was actually a venomous sting. In front of him lay a copy of the novel *A Moment of Love* by the novelist S. and two slim folders. On the cover of one was written 'S' in large black letters and on the other one in the same handwriting 'A.H. or A.F.'. I realised that these files were the young woman novelist's and mine, which had recently been opened.

'Sit down, Farfar.'

I sat down silently, trying to appear as calm as he was.

'Where's your military ID?'

'In my pocket, sir.'

'Give it to me.'

I removed it from my shirt pocket, into which it routinely hopped without my being conscious of that whenever I changed clothes. I was doubtless being arrested. There is something really different about arresting someone who is used to arresting others and about intimidating someone who has intimidated other people. My supervisor took the card from my hand, examined it, ascertained that it was still valid, and placed it in my file.

Then he asked me point blank, 'Do you know why I have summoned you, Sergeant Abdullah?'

'No, sir. I have no idea.'

'Do you see these files?'

He was fiddling with the two files, and a serpent's venomous smile shone from his lips. Three phones in his office began to ring at the same time, but he didn't reach for any of them.

I have no idea? Actually, I have a thousand.

'I am going to tear up your file right now in exchange for you stuffing her file so full it will take two men to carry it. That holds as well for the files of 'The Slaughtered Bird' and of every woman and man you come across. Record everything – even the brand of shampoo she uses, the kind of nail polish she prefers . . . everything, every last detail. Keep track of her emotions . . . her feelings.'

I rose, suffering from sudden attacks of nerves, stomach cramps, heartburn, and indigestion. I wasn't hungry even though I hadn't eaten for hours. In a feeble voice I replied, 'I'm not in the service, sir.'

'No, you are in the service, the superior service. You have been promoted, Farfar. Your rank and salary have been upgraded, and . . .'

'How about my wooden leg, sir?'

I interrupted him in an even feebler voice, sensing that I was about to pass out; I felt exactly the way I had the day I learned that the novelist A.T. had betrayed me and stolen my character al-Mudallik, but my supervisor kept talking and nails kept puncturing my skull.

'Go to Sergeant T.; he will give you your new contract and your new ID. Go! Your leg is excellent, especially when you take it into coffeehouses and clubs. I also think that your imagination has improved a great deal.'

As I staggered out of his office I heard paper ripping and three phones ringing at the same time. My leg was excellent, because I could hobble with it down danger's path. My imagination had been trained by my writing career, which had just expired in the cradle, and by all the efforts of the novelist A.T. to nurture my larvae until they developed into adult insects. I was standing on the street feeling quite queasy and holding a huge bag that contained my things when a taxi belonging to our agency and driven by a young agent I had trained stopped beside me. The driver got out, took the bag from me, put it in the vehicle, and held the front door for me while I clambered in.

He was saying, 'Greetings, Uncle Abdullah. Have a happy day, sir.'

*Chapter Nineteen*

Panting and dripping with sweat, I started to remove my growing collection of books from my bookcase. I couldn't remember which shelf I had reserved for the many novels I had planned to write during the period when I had glowed incandescently: *Four Medals and al-Mudallik, Honoured and Dead, A Theft in Broad Daylight, The Story of an Apple,* and *Prisoners in a Dungeon.* These were all eye-catching titles, and the characters were rich and inspired: al-Mudallik, my aunt's husband, the gravedigger who was also a cheerleader for a soccer team, the coffeehouse proprietor who was either a masochist or a sadist and who would demand an unruly imagination to write about him, whichever he was. I had before me dozens of pieces of paper that I had filled with writing in which I mixed reality and imagination, or so I thought. I had added special vocabulary learned from months of concerted effort. These were certainly not just grubs. I knew they weren't, and the novelist A.T. would realise that too, because I had compared them with numerous pages of the books that I was now purging. I didn't know in what neglected corner of my house I would store them. I found that my writing was about on a par with these books. The black walkie-talkie, which had been made in China, was blabbing non-stop, talking about a small flood that had occurred in the working-class neighbourhood of Jabir, where the break in the water line had finally been brought under control, about a scamp who had appeared in some of the streets of the capital distributing leaflets critical of the government while our scamps pursued him intrepidly and had almost done away with him.

Suddenly I heard a shrill voice shout, 'A.H— A.F., state your location and current activity.' So, feeling apprehensive, I stopped removing books from the shelf, straightened up, and grabbed the device. I replied, 'Yes, sir. I'm in the swamp . . . disposing of rotten eggs.'

The voice replied, 'Copy. Thanks.'

Unfortunately the swamp was my own house, which actually seemed to me at that moment to be a swamp. The books were the rotten eggs I was disposing of while I almost wept.

The old television, which had returned to daily service, was on, tuned to the local channel. Al-Mudallik, my aunt's husband, was leaping from the roof of a tall residence after drinking a bottle of the soft drink Nani. 'You all leap! You can leap now! Nani – a symbol of strength!' This was al-Mudallik's third ad for the Nani firm. I imagined two airline tickets protruding from his pocket and a green voucher (bearing the Etihad Airways logo) for the Ghulum Ikhlasi Hotel. My aunt will be grasping his hand with a besotted air comprised of an embarrassed look and a shy smile.

I finished taking the books out of the bookshelf and moved it with difficulty, even though it was empty. I stowed it under my bed after dismantling it. I carried the books to stuff them beside it, and removed the piece of paper I was using as a bookmark in a book I was absorbed in reading. It was a novel, which had been translated from English, about the war in Iraq. The heroes were three black U.S. Marines who suddenly found themselves devastated by a war that seemed pointless to them. They would sit every night gazing at the darkness, weeping for their past lives.

When I returned home yesterday with my new rank and kit and with a mind that had been reset at zero, I felt an urge to go to Qasr al-Jummayz. I wanted to bid it farewell in the guise of an author of larvae that were on the verge of becoming mature insects. Before I return to what I had been before, I wanted to see the novelist S. as a writer and not a 'mark' and her companions as respectable men of culture rather than as suspects. As for the Ethiopian waitresses who are most alluring when they butcher the language – I would no longer notice their broken Arabic, because that's not considered a breach of security.

The novelist S. was there, jubilantly cradling a copy of her book. The young man with dishevelled hair and a pencil behind his ear was present too, and the thin fellow who always carried two books appeared. I had seen him taking photos of the novelist at her book-signing. He had brought the two books this time as well. I saw an elderly short story writer who had disappeared for a number of years. It was said that he had given up reading and writing or evaluating his experiences during that period. I knew he had been in prison. A modernist poet, he was flirting with one of the Ethiopian waitresses, even as his cigarette burned.

'Your friend has shown up again,' the novelist S. called out joyfully, her blue silk head-covering lying carelessly on her shoulders, when she saw me stagger in.

'Which friend?'

'The Master, Brother. What's wrong with you, Abdullah? Do you feel sick? He has finished his new novel but refuses to tell us about it. He's been searching for you.'

That's great! The traitor has finally appeared after working for three weeks to produce his plagiarised book. Three weeks isn't long, of course, but the magnitude of the inspirations I naively provided him, along with the ins and outs of the character, charged him up and allowed him to write with incredible speed. He disappeared the day of the demonstration without taking leave of me. No doubt the demonstration was the initial catalyst for him to flee and begin writing at once. What does he want from me? Can he look me in the eye? If I were in his place, I would never show my face in public again. I would remain in hiding forever. I would write in hiding and publish from hiding and conduct interviews with journalists from behind a curtain. How do you suppose he will confront me? Will he tell me about his new novel, or will he just have me read my grubs while he sits with me in al-Bi'r Coffeehouse, lending me one ear and reserving the other for the men of the desert or the rowdy country bumpkins or possibly for another African woman who is weeping for a rebel lover? I will meet *with him but be very cold, because he means nothing to me anymore. From today on, I'm no longer a writer; I just execute orders and am now what I used to be. Even my yellow paper is no longer inspirational and instead longs for the old form of writing.*

'Where is he now?'

'Today he is very busy and has many appointments, but he'll wait for you tomorrow at your customary spot.'

Why has he left me a message? Why didn't he phone me directly? He knows my number very well. Is he ashamed to talk to me?

I found that I had unconsciously brought out my mobile phone. I rang him and heard the boring recorded message about the subscriber being unavailable and asking me to try later, and thank you. Always, thank you.

It was almost noon. I could tell this clearly from my new Bati watch, which I didn't like and which seemed to me to resemble nothing so much as a foreign body wrapped around my wrist, which was accustomed to wearing my West End watch that had shattered. The TV was still on. Al-Mudallik's ad for Nani had been repeated a number of times, and with each airing, my hatred for the ad, al-Mudallik, and the soft drink, which was mint extract that made me sick to my stomach, increased. 'I've made it to television, Farfar!' He had been happy to arrive there and had added a new pendant to his chest: a rubber bottle of the drink Nani. Any crazy fool could get on TV. The walkie-talkie was also on and continued to blabber away non-stop: 'The little birds of paradise were eaten by hawks, alas. The desert nomads have settled and the city dwellers are camping in the desert. This evening is the wedding party of the idiot and the woman who owns a beauty parlour. Be alert.' Then the shrill voice screamed, 'A.H. . . . A.F., have you wiped out all the eggs?'

Standing at attention, I replied, 'All gone, sir. All of them.'

I turned off the TV and the walkie-talkie. I didn't carry a single page of the ones that I had written and that I had been expecting to dazzle the novelist with which would make him die from shame and regret about his theft. Actually, I had torn up those pages, considering them rotten eggs just like the books. *I will go to meet the Master without any sore feelings and try to be the person he knows. I'll tell him: 'I haven't written anything and stopped reading during your absence.'* He had become a target but must not suspect he was one. I stood in the street waiting for any form of transport, only to find that a taxi belonging to our agency had suddenly stopped beside me.

The driver accosted me with a smile. 'Congrats on destroying the rotten eggs, Uncle Abdullah. Have a happy day. Get in.'

*Chapter Twenty*

The proprietor of al-Bi'r Coffeehouse was standing at the entrance with his tunic hiked up above his knees. He was speaking with shrill feminine rage with one of the many women who sell tea throughout the capital. She apparently wished to ply her trade in front of his coffeehouse. The woman was herself screaming argumentatively at him and seemed even coarser than he was. She almost threw him to the ground when she shoved him. I stood between them at just the right moment to support the proprietor of the coffeehouse and keep him from falling. Then other people suddenly assembled. The woman finally bowed to our requests, gathered up her effects, and decamped to another place. Lifting his tunic even higher and shaking off the dust from the woman's hand, he said, 'Thanks, Woody. Your coffee today is on me – yours and your friend's. By the way, Satan's waiting for you inside.'

He was known as Satan to the proprietor of the coffeehouse, who was either prey or predator, and 'the Master' to his troupe at Qasr al-Jummayz. He had been mine too but as of yesterday had become 'The Slaughtered Bird', ever since I received my new duties and returned to zero.

A number of desert men were clumped together on the floor in a corner watching an episode of the programme 'Call of the Desert' on the Crystal big-screen television suspended from the ceiling. It hadn't been there the last time. It must have been installed recently in response to customer demand. Three northerners, wearing brief tunics and white shorts were busy trying to pluck the strings of a tambour that one of them was holding. A beggar in shabby clothing was holding out a hand to beg for alms, but no one gave him anything. The novelist A.T. was sitting at our usual table with a medium-sized white packet and an ashtray filled with cigarette butts in front of him. I headed toward him and he rose to embrace me warmly.

'Harfash-Farfar, it's been a long time. I've missed you, man.'

I feigned warmth in the embrace and tried as best I could to forget that he was the target of an investigation. I didn't hold any grudge against him about writing now that I had withdrawn from the field. I would bless the stolen novel for him. I would merely censure him for disappearing the day of the demonstration without telling me – when I was his closest friend.

He sat down and so did I. I started the conversation. 'Is this reasonable, Master? You disappear without telling me? I searched for you like a madman.'

'Don't be angry, Friend. I behave erratically when the moment to write arrives. Believe me, I didn't mean any offense. Ever since I started writing I've always been like this; I can't change.'

'Never mind. Never mind. Have you completed your new novel?'

I asked this in a low, calm voice, not feeling at all queasy, although I had felt sick repeatedly during the previous days, lying in the hospital with stomach cramps after collapsing. My return to the service, which had occurred yesterday, had served as a magic potion that had ended every symptom of my intestinal upset. The proprietor of the coffeehouse came to our table, bringing my coffee himself, and placed it in front of me. Then he leaned over to touch my vile leg as he had done routinely every time I visited his coffeehouse. I had never stopped him. Instead I had allowed him to do that without objection.

'Of course I've produced it and with a strange speed. You'll really like it. Actually it concerns you personally. You're the one who inspired me to write it.'

As he said that, his hands were playing with the parcel in front of him. I knew for certain now that I had actually inspired it. He had said so himself: a rich character who had been handed to him on a golden platter. How could he not have written it in three weeks when it was as good as already written. *I know, A.T. I know, Master. But regardless of that, I'm not angry at you.*

I said, 'I wouldn't have suspected that you would write about the character of al-Mudallik, my aunt's husband, when I had told you I would write about him. And I read you the beginning of it; you said it was a larva that was worth a second look. Do you remember?'

He was watching me with an astonishment that I could discern clearly in his eyes now that I had returned to meticulous investigations again. The pupils of his eyes widened a little, his eyelashes lifted noticeably, and his eyebrows were arched. I felt even more astonished than he was.

'Al-Mudallik, your aunt's husband, the cheerleader who was a gravedigger, and the other strange characters have lost their hold on me, because I have used characters like them in my previous novels, as you know. I'm always searching for something fresh in every text I write. You appeared in my life suddenly, and we became friends with strange rapidity. Your character made me want to write about it. You are the protagonist of my new novel, Farfar-Harfash.'

'Me?'

I was conscious of a bitter taste in my gullet – the coffee that the predator-prey had himself brought me lacked any sweetness, even though I had seen him put five full spoons of sugar in it. I was shocked and realised that I had been very unfair to the novelist, and that the parasite of my service, which the Christian who ran the A'laf Bookstore had mentioned, had definitely not died during these last months. I couldn't add another word: 'Me?'

'Yes, you. I wrote about you with great enjoyment. I created a past, present, and future for you – mixing equal parts of reality and imagination. Do you know where

I've been living all this time? You'll be amazed. I rented a watchman's room in the stadium near your house and paid rent on another one, where I slept. I wanted to be near the place of inspiration to help my writing. You'll find that you're another Farfar in my novel. He has aspects of you and things that aren't you. Thank you, Farfar-Harfash. I thank you with all my heart and dedicate the novel to you, even though I haven't written a dedication to anyone.'


'By the way – don't be angry when at the end of the novel you see that I've had you return once more to the service. You infiltrate the group of people who knew you as a writer and someone who loves writing; then you write reports about them. This isn't the truth, as you know. It's imagination, which I've told you about for such a long time, the imagination that gives flavour to writing. I thought that made a really good ending. Now I'll read you the first chapter – just the first – and leave you in suspense until the book is published.'

He opened the white packet and took out a set of white pages elegantly written in black. I was near a total collapse but was able to see the title page:

The Grub Hunter

A Novel

*About the Author*

AMIR TAG ELSIR, also written as Amir Taj al-Sir, is a poet, novelist, and medical doctor born in 1960 in northern Sudan.

He studied medicine at Tanta University in Egypt and at the British Royal College of Medicine. Since then, he has published over 20 books consisting of novels, biographies and poetry collections. His novel *The Grub Hunter* (2010) was shortlisted for the International Prize for Arabic Fiction in 2011 while his 2013 novel, *366* was among the winners of the 2015 Katara Prize for the Arabic Novel. Elsir currently works as a medical doctor in Doha, Qatar.

*About the Translator*

WILLIAM M. HUTCHINS was born in 1944 in Kentucky, USA. Majoring in art history at Yale University, he graduated in 1964. His best-known work is his translation of the Cairo Trilogy by Naguib Mahfouz. He is currently a professor in the Department of Philosophy and Religion at Appalachian State University in North Carolina.

Printed and bound by CPI Group (UK) Ltd, Croydon, CR0 4YY
20/01/2026
02039280-0001